Urban Prey

See, you're called up for the two years' National Service at eighteen. If you're lucky, like me, you miss out on a war, because they don't have one going at the time. They call that your Alpha. But then, if you're out of work – and who isn't these days? – they call you up again a few years later. For the twelve months of Beta service. Brother, you know that if they call you up when you've been out of work a few years, they're going to send you somewhere on a one-way trip. Like the German Line, or Palestine or The Horn. It's a ticket to hell.

Also in Arrow by Peter Beere

TRAUMA 2020: BOOK 1

Urban Prey

Peter Beere

ARROW BOOKS

Arrow Books Limited
17-21 Conway Street, London W1P 6JD

An imprint of the Hutchinson Publishing Group

London Melbourne Sydney Auckland
Johannesburg and agencies throughout
the world

First published by Arrow 1984

Set in A.M. Compset by
Photobooks (Bristol) Ltd.

Made and printed in Great Britain
by Anchor Brendon Limited, Tiptree, Essex

ISBN 0 09 934780 6

BOOK ONE

ONE

What a damnawful night. God, what a night. It could have been the middle of a wicked winter.

It was a gelid, sopping thing, as raw and ragged as a half-healed knuckle. A night fit to freeze the brass monkeys off any cheerful thought. If you could manage to find one. The kind of night when meek, quiet people like you and me get killed. Murdered in our beds. Run down in the streets.

I crammed my hands into dampening overcoat pockets and shivered down my length. Great flaming omen this is, I thought. Morosely I waited for a long knife in the back. It was that sort of night. My galloping misanthropy unfolded until it embraced the entire, rotten, cursed world. I even hated Snoopy.

To make it worse, I wasn't even obliged to be here. I mean, I could have been doing something else. Something really useful, and safe. Filing my nails maybe on a piece of old pumice. Or darning my shirts.

I snorted. Sure, I had a choice. Either I could continue through the arrangement and probably get myself killed. Or I could pack up my troubles in my old kit bag and go home. In which case Franklyn would probably kill me.

Not Franklyn himself, he's a weedy little bozo who couldn't scare the bejasus out of a novice nun. But he has tall, muscly buddies. No, he wouldn't do anything like that really, but I wouldn't like to let him down. All conscience, that's me.

Funny how easy it is to be talked into things you don't want to do. I suppose the offer of money helps a lot. It's hard to turn it down when cash is scarcer than a virgin in a brothel.

It must have been about ten in the evening. I can't say exactly because the last watch I had was made out of plastic and you had to turn the hands yourself. I kept hoping someone would buy me one for Christmas, but twenty years later I'm still waiting.

No two ways about it, this was a hell of a place to loiter. Behind me was a graveyard. On the other side of the road, a factory on night shift. Both had been condemned about forty years ago. The factory because it was falling to bits, the graveyard because kids kept digging the coffins up. But nobody bothered much. Let's face it, when you live in this part of London nobody gives a monkey's. Even the monkeys don't care.

I stared up at the factory. From every dripping orifice, and believe me there were more than a few, decay ran wild like the rabid pox of the gods, and milky steam gobbed out like the clammy, fetid breath of unhealthy demons.

Inside was the Inferno.

Yammer yammer yammer, into the night, into the morning, into the bloody afternoon. Forever and ever. Ah-bloody-men.

I gagged on the thick stink, rich as the mouldering hot air that the coffinworms breathe, fat on the close fresh death of graves. But this was the smell of the ailing meat factory, where sightless worms daily descend into the Inferno. Big, sluggish, bipedal worms.

Flaccid and greasy and colourless from their unhealthy toil. But we call these worms men.

I was really in a cheerful mood, as you can see. I pressed my handkerchief into my face to relieve the smell.

I have always possessed two morbid fears. One is the fear of death. The other, of staying alive. Tonight I couldn't decide which was preferable. To cap it all, I realized I was dying for a crap.

Of course, right at that moment, the van pulled up. I say 'the' van, although actually it was 'a' van. I mean it was so dark it could have been anything. It even looked a bit like a moose when I squinted.

It was dark brown, which in the night, because there are no street lights in this area, looked any deep colour you could name. I could see that there was paler lettering on the side, but don't ask me to tell you what it said, it was just a smudge of paler lettering as far as I could see. When I got a chance to look in daylight, it had all been stripped off. I think it was something governmental.

Of course nobody thought to let on to me. Like shouting out, or flashing the lights or something. It could have been anybody parked there revving the engine like a madman. Could have been a busload of murderers.

I stayed put. Better than being press-ganged for the Canal. Believe me, I was pretty nervous; there was no way I was going to leave that cemetery gateway until I was sure. You wouldn't believe the battle that was going on in my belly, between my brain and my bowel.

Finally, after about two months, someone thought to make enquiries. 'Jesus Christ Beekay, are you there or what?' Beekay, that's me by the way. B. K. Howard.

I didn't recognize the voice, but it seemed familiar enough with me, so I stepped out into the full glare of the dancing night. The rain was thundering down. Actually there was thunder as well, but that was way off, over the city. It took about two seconds, maybe less, for me to be soaked to the skin like a dunked rat.

'Come on you skulkin' bugger, we haven't got all bleedin' night!'

People have the patience of saints, do you know that? Constipated saints with piles and migraines. I sort of skipped to the door of the van; I wanted to get out of the rain but I was a bit disabled by the cramps in my bum. Then with commanding nimbleness I tripped on the step and fell in a great heap, half in the doorway, half in the streaming gutter. An explosion of wind ripped out of my backside.

I picked myself up like a kid with some sort of really pathetic apology and slid the door shut. But the stinging rain on my face continued undiminished. There was no damn side window, just a gawking hole where the glass should have been. It didn't surprise me. I was going to die from pneumonia, I knew I was.

I didn't have a chance to say hello to Franklyn. He was busy throwing up into a plastic bag. Loudly. Turns out he's a lousy traveller. Gets sick just walking through a car park.

I'm trying to make light of this, but really I wasn't far from tears. I could feel them straining in my throat, buzzing in my eyes. I mean, this isn't me at all. What the hell am I doing here? Oh Jeez, this is really awful. With worse to come.

The van pulled away. Franklyn handed me his plastic bag. 'Throw that out will you Beak.' And it wasn't a question, he just took it for granted. Franklyn had some really disgusting habits. In fact, everything about Franklyn was pretty disgusting.

Like a fool I took it, between horrified fingertips. It was all hot and damp. What had he been eating for God's sake? It looked like rice pudding and peas. Some of it spilled on me. Honest to God . . .

I threw it out and tried not to scream. I wish I was a girl; they can just burst into tears and nobody minds.

Away we went, out of London, heading east. A bold band of brave buccaneers, burgeoning through the benighted black Stygian gloom.

The bollocks we were. A more inimical crew you couldn't wish to meet. There was Franklyn in the middle like a dwarf with St Vitus, the huge Negro driver, Everton, crunching mammoth gobstoppers on the outside, and me, seventy-three inches of scrawny, sodden dismay, being rained on, squashed against the door. A picnic it wasn't.

We were on our way to pick up a load of what Franklyn calls 'buggy', somewhere on the wiggly bit of the Essex coast. The police call buggy black-market stuff and try to take it away from you. So we hadn't told them we were going to collect it.

Don't misunderstand me, I'm no criminal, no common Mohock blowing in the face of an unsympathetic society. At least I wasn't then. I just needed the money. I was liable to the common conviction that cheating the government isn't entirely criminal, it's just slightly shady. And like I said, I needed the loot. Three hundred pounds. Not a lot, with cigarettes at three pounds a pack, but better than a gutful of wind.

You might wonder why the big F wanted me along.

I've often wondered that myself. I think it's because he was my uncle. Joe Family and all that.

Me, I have no such scruples. I wouldn't have taken Franklyn along if it had been my caper.

Anyway, Franklyn really bugged me. I was twenty-six then, moody, miserable, morose and misunderstood, and everybody bugged me. I was also jobless, property-less, penniless, a bit thick and I had no balls. Of course, in the year 2020 that's a way of life. You're listening to one of the proverbial poor. Easy enough to find – you look for the poverty line and we're about two feet below. Me, and about fifteen million other buggers.

Of course that's only the inside of me and may be difficult to picture. Outwardly I was much as I am now: gaunt, willowy, a touch anaemic, with a face like the villain in a cheap play. I have dark hooded eyes, a tight mouth, spikes of sparse stubble around the lips and jaw, and long, thin bones that creak. A real Adonis. In the winter my nose runs, in the summer I get hay fever and I have a squint.

But next to Franklyn, I'm an angel. Franklyn is an ugly man. Ugly, ugly – man. A real archetype. A pug would look down its nose at him. And believe me, I'm flattering the man. He stands five feet two in his highest heels. He's round. Round in the head, round in the body, round in all the corners. And of course clothes aren't made spherically, so there is always a bit, halfway down his shirt maybe or in the middle of his fly, where the buttons don't quite reach their holes. And in such unsavoury regions the eye is inevitably drawn to a shred of grubby vest or underpants, sticking out like the dough from some bulging baker's oven.

To give substance to this pregnant geography there lurks a world of bubbling fat. Floppy, elastic stuff that bestows anile breasts that would grace a Rubens, urns of alabaster thigh wobbling atop Grecian plinths, cheeks like bloated udders.

Like a simmering oven, that fat generates heat, so Franklyn sweats a lot. By a lot I mean like constantly. In the bath, in a blizzard, frozen in a block of ice, Franklyn sweats. Not a polite, delicate sheen. Franklyn sweats huge globules, like blains. Baubles which wobble on a skin the tan of uncooked chicken. Which glisten in the caterpillar tickler that crawls over his upper lip. And trickle off his chin.

Poor old Uncle Frank. He makes you want to bury him, he really does. He's a good organizer though.

The third member of our soirée, the Negro Everton, I never really got to know too well. He didn't speak much, just crunched a lot of gobstoppers.

For a while none of us said anything. Franklyn was feeling too ill and me and Everton hadn't been introduced. That suited me fine, I don't think I want to know people who blow their nose in the palm of their hand.

You may think I felt very guilty about what we were doing, that I disliked the dishonesty. Nah. I just felt bloody terrified. I really didn't want to get caught. I couldn't give a frig for the morals.

I had the feeling we were riding a timebomb. For a start we were the only damn vehicle out on the damn streets. I mean, how would you feel? The damn traffic curfew starts at six; we weren't even supposed to be travelling without an official pass, let alone driving to pick up a load of buggy. And I knew damn well Franklyn didn't have a pass. And I was pretty sure Everton didn't. I mean, they just don't give important things like that to guys who suck gobstoppers.

We were asking for it. I kept telling myself, Franklyn must know what he's doing, it's not the first time he's done this. But I couldn't convince the wobblies in my gut. I knew I was destined for bad luck. I'm always destined for bad luck. Boo hoo, poor me.

I'd never done anything wrong before, that's the trouble. Well, I once groped around with a girl called Annabel Dupont when we were about ten. I don't know if that's against the law. And I've nicked a couple of things. But you weren't likely to get beaten up and sent to gaol for that, were you?

Actually, I didn't mind going to gaol so much. It was the beating I didn't need.

These days they probably wouldn't even bother with gaol. Straight on the Ditch, that's where we'd go. God, that would just about kill Franklyn. He'd be able to fill it with his sweat.

It wouldn't do me a lot of good either. Yes sir, I had a bundle of cheerful thoughts to accompany me on this recherché journey.

Fuel is like gold dust these days you know. Any fuel. Even coiled-up elastic bands. They say that in another five years there won't be a single private vehicle left. God, you ought to see the scrapheaps coming out of London. They're like mountains, they block out all the sky. It's really eerie.

I'd never seen the area before, it really snowed me. For mile after mile, metal edifices rearing at the disinterested gods. Like a tourist attraction. (Apparently they come in droves in the summer.)

A flowerbed it wasn't. Well, a modern flowerbed maybe. A flowerbed à la homo sapiens discardus.

It's too big to call a work of art.

The construction grows out of the ground in a way

no building with its connate rigidity could. Here there is movement, a swaying, willowing, susurration and sibilance. Here are Chaos and Order melded, a virgin galaxy coalescing out of the scattered homo dust, twinkling in the dark void of Essex night. Smug.

No wonder the scene inspired the deaf and dumb poet J. J. Hangerman to pen those unimmortal lines:

> When all is dead that went before
> those vehicle mounds will endure. For sure.

Doesn't take much to become a poet, does it?

On both sides of the road we were following, ahead of us and arear, lay the ominous, uneasy, slumbering beasts. We moved, for all the world, through a delitescent herd.

The mythical They reared their anonymous heads in my muggy mind. For this was their doing. Their stillborn brainchild. Their Judas offering to the gods of Chaos.

It probably began with a simple spadeful of earth. 'Put the hole here boys!' someone had cried, ramming home a blood-dipped wooden stake. 'Take it down until you can see the bottom. Hah hah hah hah!'

They had dug out vast lunar pits, sacking the stubborn beds of clays and silt, making enormous empty lakes that should have been teeming with fish. But instead of water they'd filled in with old vehicles, ambulances, fire engines, army trucks, refuse collectors, invalid cars, coaches, street sweepers, cycles, delivery vans, recovery vans, transporter wagons, container wagons, cars, millions and millions of broken cars, seized up like so many unburied heart attacks.

When the pits were full they carried on dumping, stacking, reinforcing, buttressing – up and up, like a coral island, up and up like a jackpot spewing out, up and up, stairway to heaven. God must be a scrap-metal dealer.

What colours! What strange-sounding songs lamented the lazy teetotal wind as it sought a refuge from the tippling drunkard rain. What myriad empty eyes were scouring the empty landscape!

Franklyn told me that people even live in there. Junk City they call it. Cave dwellers. Boot dwellers. Front-seat dwellers, back-seat dwellers. Curled-up-in-the-fuel-tank-of-a-Jumbo-jet dwellers. What a life hey?

He said that some people even survive off the scraps of food lost beneath seats and rubber mats, off the water left in bottles and rads; they never leave the place. They are nomads shifting from car to truck, from truck to car. If you got lost in the middle of one of the piles you might never get out.

Junk City. What a God-damned place.

It was late now. Or early, depending how you view these things.

Anyway, Franklyn was blabbering on, as is his wont. Franklyn jabbers constantly when he's not being sick and has honed the art of repetition to the point of murder.

'What a night hey, buddy? What a night.' Pause. 'What a fuggin' night.' He popped a strong mint into his mouth and ruminated sagaciously. 'Sod me.' He yawned. 'Sod me.'

Then he turned to me and fixed me with the slightly misty-eyed avuncular look he adopts when he's feeling particularly dolorous. 'Wanna mint son?' No thanks. He kept them in the same pocket as his hanky. I saw that

16

a pimple at the corner of his mouth was about to erupt.

'Not many of us nice guys left now Beekay, d'you know that?' I shrugged. I'm very noncommittal when I'm in the mood. 'Nah. Not many of us left. All chewed up. All the nice guys got chewed up.' He offered a mint to Everton. 'Wanna mint, nignog? No? Suit yourself.' He lit a butt, hawked up a lump of phlegm and spat it past my face through the window that should have been there.

'Only crooks left now Beak. Crooks and bastards. You an' me Beak, that's all's left. Crooks and bloody bastards, buddy. Ain't that right, Everton!' he bellowed at the black man as if negroism is automatically allied to deafness, stupidity and other people's children.

'Up your ass,' came the laconic reply.

'Look at it. Like a fuggin' cemetery.' Franklyn flicked his butt after the phlegm, spraying my cheek with sparks. He was referring to the deserted townships we eternally passed through. 'Ain't no life in the country no more. No one's got no spirit any more.' It struck me as a perceptive comment for Franklyn, I wondered how he intended it. For all the spirit had gone from people, crushed by an ever more oppressive government, by the relentless, sapping war in Europe, by the poverty, by squalor, by the remorseless winter of decay. The entropy of a society. Did even coarse, uncultivated, self-regarding Franklyn, Franklyn the ubiquitous Philistine, notice it?

'I didn't know it bothered you.'

'It don't Beak. Sod me, it don't.' Another mint flew against the back of his mouth. 'It's just sometimes it annoys me.' A pause. 'Know what I mean?' He changed the subject. 'Seems to me, there's a hell of a lot more rainy days than there aren't. In a year that is. Seems to me, the world's getting wetter. Seems to me, if we ain't careful, the sea's gonna rise up and wash us all away.'

I wasn't in a mood to listen to rubbish. 'Franklyn, why don't you shut up,' I said. 'Sometimes you talk a right load of balls.'

'Oh charmin', charmin',' said Franklyn, always right there with a witty riposte.

But we didn't have time to pursue the intellection further, for Everton suddenly barked, 'Trouble!'

God, my guts nearly lurched out. He hit the brake as if he'd been electrocuted. The van sailed around on the sodden road, wondered which way to proceed, settled for sideways and drifted quietly as a snowflake for about forty yards, until it ploughed into the front of a police van. There was a horrible orchestration of breaking glass and crunching metal. Unfortunately the two dingoes had the presence of mind to leap out as we approached, and they didn't look overly pleased. In fact one of them was screaming at us. And it wasn't the King's English. All the words had only four letters. Apart from bastards.

His mate was none too chirpy either. He'd twisted an ankle and got mud all over his trousers. It wasn't a pretty sight. His expression that is.

'Goddamn crap!' cried the muddy one and he slammed his helmet down on the road. 'Goddamn damn damn damn!' He kicked the front of our van for good measure.

The other man was more attentive. 'Gerrout!' he shrieked. Even through the black visor his face looked purple. 'Out out out out *out*!' He brandished a rifle for emphasis.

These were the Pox. Officially, the Police Auxiliary. The hardest buggers they can squeeze into the jet-black

18

macho uniforms. You have to pass a really stiff test before they'll take you in the Pox. You have to have your brain excised.

Scared? Me? I wet myself. It's a few years since I've done that. The smell is appalling. Not to mention the embarrassment. I was so scared I even began to cry. I'm not cut out for the rough stuff.

'Against the van! Against the van!' They frisked me gently, the way a rutting buffalo might.

Then they flung us all about a bit, just to keep in shape. They threw us into the mud, across the bleeding road. Bounced us around amongst the potholes. Then we were slammed against the van again. My nose started to run.

'Wassina van? I said, wassina fuggin' van?' before anyone could answer.

'Sausages!' shouted Franklyn thickly. It was so ludicrous I choked. 'It's a load of bloody sausages! Take a look!'

The guy slowed down. You could hear his brain struggling to make sense. 'Where's it goin'?' he grunted charily. 'Lemme see your pass!' He seemed reluctant even to wait for a reply.

'I haven't got one,' said Franklyn.

Don't hit me, a little voice pleaded in my brain, like a creature in a crumbling burrow. Please please please don't hurt me. All hero, that's me.

For a moment the legalized thug seemed quite calm. For a while he forgot to shout at us. I tried to figure out what was going on behind the black, eyeless visor. I figured he must have had a stroke or something when a minute passed with nothing happening, but suddenly he

19

burst into life with a scream and a few more imprecations.

'Open the doors! I said open the goddamn doors!' He liked to repeat things. Authority thinks we're all deaf.

He shoved Franklyn to the back of the van, and none too gently. Poor Uncle Frank lost a lot of blood when his nose broke a fall. The other bully, the muddy one, kept us covered. You could see he was pretty annoyed about the mud, he kept growling and flicking at it with his tight black macho gloves. Maybe he was a faggot, I don't know.

Uncle Frank opened the double doors at the back, then – Jesus Christ the guy's head blew up. Have you ever seen a head hit by two shotgun blasts from about six feet? Believe me, a fancy black helmet doesn't help much.

God, one minute the guy's standing there, all black and manly and tough. Then there's just a body staggering back a step and a crimson volcano spewing out of the shoulders. A spray of blood and brain – spread into the night as if a balloon had burst. And dark, dark blood welled out of the cleaved neck, like ketchup boiling over in a saucepan. It was hissing where the air in his lungs struggled to the night like divers coming to the surface. I've never seen blood so, so naked, it seemed so radiant, so luminescent. So bubbling. I just screamed.

The other guy, the faggot, must have looked away for a moment; who wouldn't? Only for a heartbeat, for the quick tick of a clock. But Everton had him cold, lunging forward like a hungry dog. He swung his leg as if he was trying to vault over the bugger, but the huge boot caught him right at the base of the scrotum, drove the guy's crutch halfway into his belly, lifted him clear of the ground.

All that terrible dawn of pain made him suck in the

20

night in a great hoot, filled his lungs with a terrible darkness. He jack-knifed in the air and when he landed, still on his numb feet, still sucking in that first quick breath of vertiginous shock, he was bent forward like some ancient gigolo beseeching the thunderclap negro for a quickstep, heels together, toes apart. And Everton's ready hand slashed down. He slashed it down like a starter dropping a flag, down the side of the neck below the chinstrap, swung it under the throat, so hard, so savagely that a razor blade shattered and half of it was lost as the ruptured skin closed instantly around it, hid itself away in the flesh.

I heard the blood pump out. Like someone spitting between their teeth. Like an old man brushing his boots with slow, deliberate strokes. Great incarnadine spurts that couldn't escape quickly enough.

The dingo pitched forward, still very alive. His legs and arms began to twitch and quiver crazily, his quickstep had gone all to pieces, he was mortified. There was a dreadful, macabre scream and I thought, he shouldn't be screaming with his throat cut. But he wasn't, it was me.

The blood spread so quickly, so thickly, like vomit steaming in the night. Out past his shoulders, up past his head. He could have been trying to swim in it, to escape, and still he went on quivering and kicking, scraping his knuckles across the pitted tarmac, undressing them to the bone. I thought he'd never stop. And he vomited. All this fried potato and egg came up, a great pulpy yellow mass, smothered in steaming red sauce.

I threw up.

And somehow it was all so silent. All so slow. A mime of death.

I was a spectator at a ballet. A bloody ballet, of commonplace death. Someone slapped me to shut me up.

They hid the bodies, Franklyn, Everton and the two guys who had been in the van. They might have been changing a tyre.

They rolled the crippled police car aside, pocketed the guns. Talked over the blood as if it could tell them something. Someone said, 'This is Midge and Deko.' They were old men. I didn't bother saying hello. I was still gibbering.

I didn't want any of this violence. All I wanted was some money. Like a small boy. I told myself, over and over, peering ahead through bloodshot brimming eyes as the van pulled away, all I want is the money. All I want is the money.

I had to get away. Out of England. West of course. No point going east, into the war. The bloody desultory war that trailed on for months and years until everyone was numbly sick of it and all the excitement and fear had gone.

West, across the grey Atlantic, that was the way to go. Out of this squalor, into their squalor. At least it was different.

But it cost nothing to stay. To go cost money. Lots of money, otherwise everybody would go. The country would scarper.

Needed money. Money money money. Need to work for Franklyn.

He'd let me down. The bastard had pushed me off the plank, the way uncles do when you're a green kid. I felt a gall of hate and bitterness heave up in me. If he'd touched me I would have thrown his hand off like a great betrayal, I would have cried out in the voice of a bewildered child. I was tense and brittle, fighting hard to stay at least outwardly rational. I was chomping on my teeth, making all the unhealthy roots ache.

We were all quiet. Funereally quiet. I don't know what the other two were thinking but Everton seemed to be crunching more pensively on his gobstopper. Perhaps he had a premonition of his own doom.

Perhaps he was upset about his razor, they're hard to get these days. Anything metallic is hard to get, it all goes on the war. It's crazy, we can't get any razor blades and there's a million or more cars lying a few miles down the road.

I'll tell you one thing I've noticed; this war has a hell of an appetite. It eats anything. Metal, paper, food, drugs, blankets, people. You name it, the war will find room for it. It's like a sacrificial idol. I thought about it to take my mind off the horror. Ironic hey?

Just as I got around to thinking, it's time the big F said something, he opened his mouth, gargled a bit of mucus and said, 'It's a right bloody night isn't it hey?' I didn't say anything.

'Yes sirree, a right bloody dingbat of a bloody night.' He hit a tangent. 'I wonder what your dad's doing now?'

'Probably in the nick. Or maybe he's on a chain gang on the Ditch, he always did like camaraderie.'

'Camaraderie?' said Franklyn as though it was a type of pizza he'd not heard about. 'Aye. But he was all right your dad.' All right. He was a drunk. A brawler. I hated his guts.

I saw him in my mind's eye. Whenever I picture my dad his face is blurred, diffused, snarling, and it's the

23

flat palm of his hand, the deformed four fingers with the cheap gold ring that I see. I duck. It's not often I conjure up my father. That's all I see, the descending palm, the fingers, the ring. He was a bastard. I hated him.

'Aye, he was all right your dad.'

Money money money, I thought. Just give me the money and let's get it over with.

After midnight we reached the target, a muddy, picayune field blown over by a smell of sewage, close by the sea.

We weren't alone; I counted a dozen other trucks, vans and pick-ups nosing about uncertainly without lights. There were a couple of bumps, a few angry exchanges. Everyone seemed to know everyone, but no one seemed friendly. Is that how business is conducted?

There was a bit of argy-bargy as the transport pack tried to force its way down a narrow incline to a flat, bushy strip of land below, where one of the many Essex inlets nibbled satedly against the scabrous crust of the land. Everton had experience of this kind of thing. Though last to arrive we were second on to the chock-a-block ramp. He had to tumble somebody out of the way to get there, but what the hell.

He pulled up right at the skirt of the water, broke off the engine and we waited. It fell very quiet when the hubbub ceased and you might have thought we were duckshooters waiting for the dawn. The rain had wandered off somewhere and scattered patches of starlight were being lowered from the balcony.

Gradually the cab filled with a marshy air. It wasn't cold but it was damp. The murmur of men in other cabs filled my head with a drone which threatened to send me to sleep. But nerves kept me awake. Couldn't relax. Needed a crap. Franklyn and Everton had flaked out immediately. The only thing that kept them from snoring was that I kept shutting their goddamn mouths. I hate to hear people snore.

Eventually I must have dropped off myself, for next thing I was waking up.

Franklyn parted his buttocks and let a clap of thunder roll into the night.

Everton jumped down. Beyond him, in the eldritch light of muted lanterns stuck on poles in the ground, I saw three low barges silently grounding on the sandy mud. Tiers of flattened, exhausted waves came in with them. I could hear voices, familiar reassuring voices – the illusion of camaraderie – murmuring like a covey of weary seabirds.

I followed Franklyn into the morn, uncreasing the dampness from my creaking legs and elbows.

Franklyn shouted something to a lazulite sailor perched on the flat top of one of the brown barges. At the same time he motioned Everton to open the van. Quite suddenly a buzz of activity rose up all around, sweeping past, like leaves that have gently drifted down a leisurely stream suddenly to encounter a tract of pebbly shallows. I stuck close to Uncle Frank.

Time to earn my smackers. A hundred and eighty bulky boxes and crates to be transferred to the van, and not a lot of time to do it. Those sailors (they seemed to be French) were pretty itchy. (I think the flat-headed guy screaming *schnell! schnell!* while we struggled to take half-ton boxes off him, was German. I thought they'd all died in the First Assault.)

It didn't take long to work up a lather. But there was no time even to take off my coat. Everything proceeded at a furious pace. Hammer hammer hammer.

(I noticed that I started wheezing as I ran short of breath. Made a mental note, must get into better shape. Knew I wouldn't.)

The underfoot degenerated quickly until it was a mire of fine, gungy mud which crept gradually higher, like a tide up our stumbling legs. It also smelt; I think maybe there's a leak in one of those sewage pipes.

It was heartbreaking stuff, after a few minutes every step became a flight of cathedral steps. All I wanted to do was lie down. But I was urged on by the haste on all sides.

Throughout all this, Franklyn remained officiously to one side, haggling over pieces of paper with the demented Frenchman who appeared to be in charge of the barge. I didn't ask what we were shifting. I didn't have the breath for one thing. But from the markings on some of the crates – most had German or Arabic designations – I guessed that at least part of the consignment was narcotics and ammunition. Deeper and deeper with every step. In more ways than one.

I wasn't accustomed to this kind of travail. I was used to idling around all day, looking through the jobsheets, swapping newspapers, rapping with my mates. Brute strength just isn't my forte. It didn't take long, four minutes maybe, for blisters to begin to rub up on my ruddy mounds. A couple of minutes later I was really cringing. Then the aches in my biceps (ha!) and calves began to knot, drew tighter and tighter until the blood had to batter a way through. Have you ever been through a sieve? I was squeezed through a bloody mincer. Twice.

26

The mud fastened on to me like a pack of leeches, sucking out all the vitality that my muscles had neglected to accrue over the years. And some bugger was rubbing a cheese grater up and down the tender flesh of my throat. If I hadn't been humiliated enough already I would have collapsed. Thank God we were almost through.

But, quite suddenly, something tugged at the sleeve of my attention. I shook my head to listen. A sound, the suggestion of a sound maybe, it wasn't very clear. Perhaps it wasn't there at all . . .

The commotion of the little crowd gathered on this stretch of English soil suddenly subsided and there was a long, long pause while everybody who wasn't deaf or stupid listened. There it was again. But what? It was very indistinct. It came from no particular direction.

It was like the clatter of a startled bird's wings.

Wary eyes looked about. A hundred men and women stared into the night. Sniffing the air like dogs. The uneasy night crowded around nervously.

Then, over a copse of treacherous trees further down the inlet, something zoomed into view like a bloody dragonfly, bright as a firefly against the lifting night. A helicopter! Jesus! All lights blazing.

At the same instant a flare shot into the sky above our heads, a bright, bright flare, hotter than magnesium, painting us all with instant platinum.

Jesus Christ, I just stopped my bowels from opening. A harsh, metallic voice screamed from the field above our heads, the field that we'd all churned up with our argy-bargy. I didn't realize at first that it was the Pox, I thought it must have been some of our guys. Christ they must have crept and trundled up that track like church mice.

But then I heard the voice crackling over and over again. 'This is the Police Auxiliary! The Police Auxiliary!'

The Police Auxiliary! I was paralysed. I was like a small boy caught with his fingers in his mother's purse. While all around other people were losing their heads, I was losing mine. I began to shout, crazily, without meaning, trying to outdo everybody else to make myself heard in this suddenly ruptured ant-nest.

Figures were darting hither and thither, cold in the bright gay light, flat as cardboard figures slid on revolving legs. Panic panic everywhere and not a pause to think.

Suddenly, right in front of me somebody – a woman I think – was shot.

All at once the whole thing leapt beyond my comprehension into nightmare. And in response the wild, crazy shouting evaporated in the back of my throat. I crouched instinctively, but it brought my face close to the bundle that an instant before had been screaming abuse at everything in sight, and I threw up.

A huge piece of her face had been taken away, her right cheek, ear, eye and a piece of jaw. I saw the bone of the skull, looking pink, struggling too late to heal itself. And there in the middle, steaming brain trickling. It looked like a mass of greyish, white worms sucking blood.

I twisted away, scrabbling towards Uncle Frank, as though I thought he could calm all this tumult, as though he was safety. For a moment it looked as though he was. He stood there like some great dictator, apparently astounded at the affrontery, looking as if he ran the show. For a moment he looked like he could stop the tide from turning.

But when I got close I saw that he was scared to death. He wasn't affronted, he was terrified; his face was twitching, dribbling like a baby. His hands were shaking, his whole body quivering like the dead poxy in the nightmare earlier. He couldn't speak to calm this terror, he couldn't even move.

I followed his gaze – there was Everton and the two old men, Midge and Deko, ripping automatic rifles from a roll of canvas in the maw of the van. I let out a scream.

'This is the Police Auxiliary. The Police Auxiliary. You have no escape. You have no escape.' The usual official nasal repetition. 'Spread yourselves on the ground. Spread yourselves on the ground face down. You will not be harmed. You will not be harmed.'

The helicopter swept down so low I caught my reflection in the polished ebony belly, white as the moon and twice as scared. The wind blasted me on to my back, Uncle Frank flopped on top of me. The din was infernal.

Everton fired, a score of bullets in the first stentorian second. The Frenchmen dug with frantic feet into the soft, bastard ooze, thumped against the low bow of the stubborn barge, pushed pushed screaming. I could see their muscles, as clear as naked men.

A crackle of guns like twigs on a bonfire. And the bonfire all around, hiding in all the lights. I scrambled up and ran, dodging through the flames, the coward in me buried beneath terror which lent me wings. I leapt over a small van and scarcely touched the roof. Louder came the gunfire, thumping. This the third second. I stopped with a gasp as someone slammed into me, then rushed off, my breath impaled upon his shoulder.

I span on a wobbly leg, crumpled on one knee while

my abdomen roared. I looked up, for a moment blinded as a second flare bowed into the fading chamber. Then I saw the cardboard characters, not the distance of a spit from me, fighting back like cornered dogs. To my left the barge crept into the tide, a foot, a yard, two yards. The Frenchman with his papers ran after his launch, one foot in the water, a leap to the gliding flat deck . . . . He died before the trailing leg left the sea, back and shoulders fulminated in a bloody spew as a cluster of slugs spattered through the flesh on their way to splinter the gunwale. A dark wave drowned the piercing shriek as his long body snapped, flung itself away from the barge in a frenetic, angry dance which took it beneath the tide. Cascades of thrashing water roiled about the spot, growing brown where the greasy effluence from the punctured corpse leaked and bubbled to the surface, steaming.

His crewmates didn't reach to help, they were dying more slowly, indulging in intricate, composite deaths of drowning and wounds, trapped on the platinum stage like actors failing their audition. Undignified deaths, loud and colourful and untidy. Coughing blood like apologies.

They didn't waste any bullets on Everton and his two buddies, sheltered momentarily by the bulk of the van. They blew it up. There was a soft, rushing thud, a flash of fire. Then the van exploded in a fulguration of red and orange flame. A genie of evil smoke gyred into the sky, a terrible dark creature shot through with veins of vermeil heat and shock. It was incensed, furious; in its brief, violent life it hated everything. Everton and the aged dwarfish companions disappeared into the night in a thousand red pieces. Half an arm landed at my feet and tapped me.

If Franklyn hadn't stumbled blindly in front of me the blast might have killed me. But he took it in my place, blast and fire, shrapnel and all. I rolled backwards in the mud, lumps of my uncle sparged all over my body like crushed fruit, the instant of his death booming cavernously through my battered brain. It burned the oxygen in my lungs, set fire to my whole inner chest. Robbed me of my sight.

I thought I was on my feet, running, fleeing, but I was scrabbling backwards on my knotted bum, pushing myself along on heels and wrists. And all the while, up above, the fiery sky that had supplanted my seared sight throbbed and screamed and tried to bring me back.

I scuttled under a van, knowing it only by the stench of oil and the piece of jagged metal that cut through my scalp like a ploughshare. I was desperate. I was fleeing like hell but the roaring, screaming furore was still around me. I wasn't getting anywhere. I'd crawled for miles but I was still in the middle of it all.

Suddenly my sight sprang back with a painful wrench at the back of my eyes, a piercing deep in the skull.

I had only scrambled about fifty yards, I could still feel the heat of the blazing van whipping the hairs off my face. Everybody was shouting and wailing, God it was like a full-scale war. The copter kept buzzing the scene, maybe it was taking pictures. I don't know. I thought, how the hell did they know we were here? But it wasn't the place for debate.

I managed to get myself right way up, on my feet and running, limping, tripping the light fantastic. They say the first step's the hardest. Not true. Every step was just as difficult. I wanted to throw my hands in the air and say: hey, look I surrender, I'm not fighting, don't hurt me. But I didn't think they'd notice. I wasn't sure they wanted prisoners. So I ran.

Then out at sea I heard a gunboat open up. They must have found the boat that brought the barges over. That settled it. I ran like a bloody gazelle, weaving, dodging, employing all those fancy ice-skating manoeuvres I've watched on TV. I became aware that someone was after me. Not pursuing, but out of all that pandemonium a voice seemed to be speaking to me. 'You there! Halt immediately! You have nowhere to go! You will be shot if you do not give yourself up!'

I saw a knob of trees and bramble jutting out from the slope, on to the ledge. That was where I was going, I had it fixed in my mind. It was only thirty yards away, I could make it easily.

I glanced over my left shoulder, back to the dark shapes of the pox on the rise. Jesus H. Christ, there was a bloody great Alsatian sprinting towards me like flaming Alecto, ripping apart the night. God, it had my number all right. No mistake, I was the one it wanted.

I was going flat out, but I redoubled my pace, fled across the ground like a scarecrow caught up in a whirlwind. I was really prancing, taking enormous, madman strides to get me to the trees on time. I risked another quick glance. Jesus Christ the dog was almost on me! I could see the colour of its bloody tongue, the firelight blazing from its eyes. Christ, why can't I run like that! They should put it on the track.

I hit the first hurdle of bramble badly, ripped through like a lunatic fleeing the asylum, picking up half-inch thorns as if I saved the bloody things. The damn dog leapt it in a bound. I heard it land on the run. It must have covered fifteen feet without any effort and it didn't even grunt.

I could feel it gathering itself. I threw myself down, buried my face in the wringing ground, clasped my hands on the back of my head.

The beast hit me like a bolide. I thought it must have splintered all my ribs. Then it grabbed hold of my left arm. The pain was incredible, I screamed like a fox at the death. A terrible, blackening pain that went thudding down to the bone – throbbing along my arm to the hand, lancing up the arm to my chest. I swirled into a dark abysmal vortex of oblivion like analgesia. It was the only good thing that had happened to me all day.

TWO

Early morning. A grey sky drained of health, emotion. It looked as sick as I felt.

I had passed through the jaws of Alecto. I had her venom in my flesh. They say that some of those police dogs are deliberately infected with a strain of rabies. I hope to God they're wrong.

My nerves followed the course of the crazed dog's savagery. Unable to rip my left arm from its socket it had taken a grip on my left leg and tried to drag me back to the beach. But aided by the paludal ground I had proved too stubborn, though it had succeeded in swinging me through ninety degrees. So it had shifted its attack to my flank, where the pain was so intense I thought a kidney had been removed without anaesthetic.

Then the dog had split my coat down the middle seam so that it could tear my shirt away for its scrapbook, and explored higher. It had bitten a chunk out of my nape, chewed on my hands. Then left. Perhaps it had gone for some tools, I don't know.

I woke up crying.

After the pain the first thing I noticed was the silence. And the smell. I think the dog had peed on me, marking me. Maybe it planned to come back. I lay there for ages. Frightened to move. Frightened to trust the voiceless dawn. Pinned down by the terrible hole in my neck.

34

The knob of trees and bramble was like a lazaretto. Nobody else seemed to be there. I had been overlooked, that's what I kept saying to myself, they've forgotten me. But I couldn't move in case I was wrong.

How long can you lie without moving? An hour maybe? That's how long I lay motionless, the only activity in my watery eyes, seeing only blood flecks on the grass and the murky sky. The pain didn't lessen, it grew worse. But it was better than, I don't know, I suppose it was better than death. Maybe.

This was a rum do. I seemed a long way from the coast of America now. The best-laid plans of mice and fools . . .

I was a fool to listen to Franklyn. Fool to listen to myself. I should have listened to Gay, she told me it was stupid. She wouldn't even talk to me for two days. What was she likely to say now? I told you so, look at the state of you . . . More likely to crack me one.

I wonder if she could hear me thinking about her? Help Gay. Help. Bring a bandage.

Cautiously, like ultra-cautiously, I raised my screaming head.

Nothing.

By nothing – no action, no imminence, no sign of life. Smoke. It looked like the stuff the low clouds were made of. I shook my senses, almost lost them. Racked myself with crimson coughing. Pulled my parts together. Slowly, very slowly, I hauled myself back the way I'd come.

With nobody about to watch I dragged my body into a reasonably erect position and staggered about a bit at the edge of the night's devastation. But, on the face of it, there wasn't a lot to see. Everything of import was in the knowledge of the cause.

35

There were no bodies as I thought there would be. There was nobody about at all. What there were, were morsels of bodies, too small or messy to be picked up easily, teeth and ears and bits of organs, scattered about like inter-tidal anemones on the mud.

The barges were there, wallowing stealthily, tethered by long ropes to trees on the rise. Presumably they'd be picked up later. Several of the vehicles were parked in a line by the ramp, probably also waiting. The rest of the motors had either been driven away or destroyed in the conflagration. I found the convulsed skeleton of our van. It wouldn't be making any more clandestine trips. All the crates had gone of course.

I looked out to sea. A couple of dawn ducks flew past, low. As brown and grey as the sky. This was it then. This is where Uncle Frank and all those other people had died. I looked around to see if there were any bits of Uncle Frank, but I couldn't recognize him. It all looked like cat food.

I took off my coat and threw it on to the tide; it was too embarrassing to wear. People were sure to ask: hey, what's all this blood and guts stuck to your coat? I knelt down at the water's edge and had a good relph.

I wasn't upset at Franklyn's death. To be honest it left me singularly unmoved. I'm not very strong on family ties. But the whole night left me sick. I mean, they weren't doing a lot of harm. Were they? Just to shoot them down like that, like dogs. Like bloody dogs.

I said to myself, if I ever find out who grassed I'll kill them. I took an oath on it. I shouted it across the water, I'll get you, you bastard! I cried, I'll get you! Childish I know, but what can you do? I was really bitter. I was sobbing like a baby.

So there I was, the great pacifist, taking a vow of

revenge and murder. I remember thinking to myself, more than half seriously, sod the pacifism, I'm going to be an anarchist. Let's face it, what can you do when you're staring down the wrong end of the barrel? Kick them in the balls and hope they miss. Get your head blown off. It's all the same.

I turned my back on the sea – there's symbolism for you – and undeterminedly set off on the long trek home. I didn't leave a little wooden cross for Uncle Frank, or anything stupid like that. I really didn't like him much. I just tried to forget the – immediacy of it all.

THREE

I've just got back to London after three days of walking
and tripping up and generally wearing myself out,
kipping in doorways and living off Mars Bars, and
there's a letter lying there, face down on the patchy
lino, daring me to not pick it up.

I live in one of the seedy bedsits you hear about, all
bed and no room to sit. My letterbox is a crack under
the door. My window is a tear in the cobwebs.

I looked out of the window before I picked up the
letter. I always judge the contents of a letter by the
weather. It was raining.

I knew before I picked it up that it was the Beta call-
up. Do you know what that is?

See, you're called up for the two years' National
Service at eighteen. If you're lucky, like me, you miss
out on a war, because they don't have one going at the
time. They call that your Alpha. But then, if you're out
of work – and who isn't these days? – they call you up
again a few years later. For the twelve months of
Beta service. Brother, you know that if they call you up
when you've been out of work a few years, they're
going to send you somewhere on a one-way trip. Like
the German Line, or Palestine or The Horn. It's a ticket
to hell.

Shit almighty. You don't get a week like this every
week of your life.

I skimmed it through. It was all there. I had to report at Woolwich in five weeks. Bring my own underwear. Here's the question that really got me, on the very bottom of the bloody form – 'Is there any reason why you should not be considered eligible or available for National Service II? If so inform the Enlistment Officer at the Camp named by . . .' and here the date was smudged. Probably expired anyway.

Any reason? Any reason? Of course there are reasons you bloody morons! I'm shit scared for one. I don't bloody want to go for another, I don't want to get fried up on some foreign field. Surely I have a right to my life. No?

Like I said, you don't get a week like this every week.

I sat down on the bed and had another little sob. It's getting to be a habit that. I'm just not cut out to deal with upsets. I have my own plans, why won't they let me get on with them?

And then I thought, hell's bells I've got to go and tell Aunt Melanie about Franklyn. Hell's bells. It never whines but it roars. I can't take all this, I'm only twenty-six I should be enjoying myself. That's a bloody laugh.

I took my little kettle and went downstairs to the kitchen to fill it. Someone had been sick in the sink, but what's new in that? I rinsed most of it away. Upstairs again and the gas was off. Dammit, the bloody gas is always going off. Hell, what are we paying all those charges on the bill for?

I had a cold wash, went without the cup of tea. Found a cleanish shirt under the pile of mags beneath the bed. I put my clothes under mags so that the mice don't eat them; they eat the paper first.

I checked myself in the tin lid nailed to the wall. One

day I'll buy a proper mirror. Gordon Bennett, look at that. The nightmares have come to town. Decided I'd better wash my hair. Used the last of the soap on my body so had to use detergent on my head. Popped a couple of pimples. Ran a comb through my lengthening stubble. Put on my best jacket. Which is also my only jacket. Just had time to stamp a roach on the way to the door.

Damn rain tippled down as I slammed the rickety door with a funereal flourish and trotted down the street. It was almost lunchtime now. A Friday.

I was lucky to have a tenny of my own. My dam had left me some dough when she moved on, not a lot, a few hundred, and I scraped the rent together out of the interest and my fortnightly 'State'. It didn't leave much for cleaning and eating and other such luxuries of the flesh, but I sneaked a hell of a lot of meals at the welfare canteen. You were supposed to have a green card for that, but there are ways of slinking in. And it's a damn sight better than living in a hostel. Believe me, I've tried a couple.

Anyway, if you could eat the welfare food you deserved to get away with it. I tripped over a piece of metal and nearly dived into a cellar full of liquid mud. So that's where they get their gravy from.

It was about a mile to Franklyn's place. The rain had passed on by the time I got there.

The pad was on the second floor of a four-storey, directly above the deaf old man with the trombone, directly below the Welsh homos who were always throwing bottles at each other. I don't know why Franklyn didn't get something better; I guess he was

40

saving his dough for something. I mean, the tenny itself wasn't bad, it's just you couldn't hear yourself think for all the din. It was like intruding, you went in on tiptoe and came out with a migraine.

It seemed very quiet today I thought as I yanked on the wire that rang Aunt Mel's bell. I hadn't been there for a while, maybe things had changed.

An upstairs window clattered in its frame and a plump peroxided head ogled down at me from rolls of neck. 'Oo-oo,' waved Aunt Melanie in case I hadn't seen her. Half of bloody London must have seen her. 'Oo-oo. I see you Bartholomew, I see you.'

This is what I dread, Aunty Melanie in a cheery mood. Aunty Mel in a miserable mood I can handle; she dissolves a couple of tranks in a glass of gin and sits snuffling in a corner for hours at a time. But Aunty Mel in a cheery mood is, well – she gets kind of frisky. If you can imagine a bale of uncongealed latex being frisky. Bartholomew by the way, that's me. Bartholomew Kafka Howard. Beekay or Beak for short.

'I'll be right down, Barty,' she sang. 'Your lovely Aunty Mel will be right down.' The last word embraced half an octave. See what I mean? I didn't dare look around in case the street was watching. I dived in as soon as the door opened. 'My, my you're eager today Barty,' said Aunt Mel with what can only be described as rapacious lust in her bloodrun eyes. 'Can't wait to get your hands on me hey?'

It's always the same when Mel gets me on her own. Hungry isn't in it. And blunt, well, the things she suggested to me when I was a little lad are enough to make the Vice Squad reach for a dictionary. Don't get the wrong idea though, we've never done anything.

41

When I was young I was too terrified, now I'm too particular. I try just to joke through it. It's kind of sad really.

Anyway, she'd probably be disappointed if she did have me. She looks a very pneumatic woman. I just gave a noncommittal kind of leery grin and preceded her upstairs, clenching my buttocks for fear she'd pinch me.

'Nice,' I said, pretending to look around. 'You've done it up.'

She looked about, bored. 'Yes. Uncle Frankie lifted a load of paint and couldn't get rid of it all. He used some up in here.'

'Nice,' I said. 'I've always liked pink and turquoise.'

Mel said nothing. She had caught sight of herself in one of the several mirrors that dazzle the room and was trying to smoothe out a few creases from her amorphous stomach. Waste of time, she's had them too many years.

She was snuggled in a fluffy pink gown which left bits of itself all over the room, and she had on turquoise slippers. Presumably to complement the paintwork, they certainly didn't complement each other. There was a white lamb stitched above her heart, leaping. She had on jangling earrings which tinkled as she moved and an assortment of cheap rings undulated on her fingers. A mock gold chain hung around her neck with the letters MEL against her throat. In case she forgets who she is.

She's fat. No two ways about it, Aunty Mel is a fat woman. Not plump or round or cuddlesome. Aunty Mel has run to fat. More than run to it, I should think she took a taxi. Most of her life is dedicated to trying to conceal it, shoving lumps into knickers and waistbands

42

and enormous bras, squeezing it from her sides around to the back, stretching her short neck upwards whenever she remembers.

But to no avail. If you sprayed her with silver she'd still look like an armoured knight. But, as they say, her heart's in the right place. Right beneath the leaping lamb. And her breath always smells sweet. She has the sweetest breath I know. I think she eats toothpaste.

'Seems a lot quieter,' I said helpfully.

'Yes, well,' purred Mel dreamily, still absorbed in the smarmy mirrors, 'that pair upstairs got evicted and the old man died. Never cleaned out his trombone, got some infection, passed on. Be warned.' What did she mean by that? 'They reckon he was there three weeks before he was found. His cat had started to eat him. That was dead too.

'I told Uncle Frank there was a funny smell in the place but he wouldn't listen. He just said I should have more baths. I mean,' she sort of twisted her shoulders a bit as if she had a ricked neck, 'I get a good bath once a month. What more can you do? He was premated.' I guess she meant cremated, though with Mel you could never be entirely sure.

'What happened to the cat?'

'Some kids had it. Said they were going to try stuffing it. Do you think this gown suits me, not too osbentatious is it?'

I shook my head. What can you say? 'I don't think it's at all osbentatious.'

'Uncle Frankie's not been back yet. He didn't take you off with him did he?'

'Off where?'

'Off wherever he went. I suppose he was going to get shot of the junk. Or off on one of his binges. He didn't

43

take you off with him did he? You're too young to start that kind of life. I don't mind the robbing but I don't want you out drinking all night.' I shook my head. 'Would you like to see what I've got on underneath?' I knew she had nothing on underneath. I'd just had a Mars Bar, couldn't risk being sick so changed the subject, got straight to the point.

'Uncle Frankie won't be coming back.'

'What do you mean, Barty?' asked several faces in mirrors. 'I don't think these slippers go.'

I cleared my throat. 'The Pox turned up. A lot of them were killed.'

The face in the mirrors was suddenly, from every angle, all alertness. I felt an ominous chill enter the room.

'Not your Uncle Frankie?'

I nodded.

She blinked a few times, turned away from the mirrors, the back of her head with the patch of white crown to me.

'Did you see him?'

I nodded.

'Was it quick?'

'As quick as could ever be. I don't think he knew.'

'Poor old Frankie.'

'He . . .' I didn't know what to say. So I said, 'He enjoyed himself.' She nodded.

'Are you all right?'

'One of their dogs chewed me up a bit,' I said, embarrassed at not being more badly hurt. 'But – I guess that's all.'

'That's good,' she said. 'That's good,' she trailed away.

A long pause followed on. She smoothed her hands

on her hips. 'I, er . . . I er . . .' she turned back to me with a damp smile. 'Would you like a drink, Barty?'

'No thanks Mel. I thought I'd just . . .' I really didn't know what I was saying so packed up. I felt terrible, really terrible. I'd never been in a spot like this before.

Then suddenly she just kind of collapsed into my arms. We clutched each other tight, tight as lovers but with a different desperation. She was sobbing, huge convulsive sobs that nearly rocked me off balance. But she did it without a sound, like she didn't want me to know.

'You wouldn't think I'd love him,' she blurted, 'would you? Big slob like that. You wouldn't think I'd love him.' She clutched me so tightly it was mangling my chest. I waited for her to say more, but she didn't, just hung on to me, rocking me from side to side like her baby.

I put my hand up to smooth her hair, and it was like a brush, so dry it almost cut me. Poor old Mel. Poor old bloody cow.

After a time she sensed my awkwardness, pulled herself together. She unwound us, wiped her eyes on her sleeve. 'I er – I guess I won't have to bother with funeral arrangements,' she said. 'That's usually taken care of isn't it? I suppose they'll take care of it.'

'Yes,' I lied, not telling her there wasn't enough of Franklyn left to be buried.

'I'd like to do something though. Maybe I'll, er, maybe I'll put an ad in the *Post*. Maybe. Or . . .' wondering, '. . . yeah I think I'll put in an ad.'

'That's a good idea,' I said earnestly. 'I think – I think that's a good idea.' I couldn't say 'he'd like that', it's so corny.

'Yeah,' said Aunt Mel. 'I'll do that. What's the time?

Maybe I can get down there now. Get it,' her voice dropped at the unconscious irony, 'out of the way.' She looked at a mirror, the clock, another mirror. 'Yeah, I'll do that.'

'What will you do?'

'I don't know. I suppose you just go down there.'

'No, I mean afterwards.'

'I dunno. See what I've got. See what I can do. I've got a cousin who gets married soon, maybe, maybe they'd like to move in with me. I don't know. I'll have to see, I'll give it some thought.'

'If you need anything –'

'Yeah, I know Barty. Thanks love. You're a good kid.' She sounded sincere, but she was beginning to busy herself now, fill her mind.

'I'll be on my way then Aunt Mel,' I mumbled. 'I've got someone else to see.'

'Sure Barty. Sure. Come by soon, we'll get drunk hey? Maybe you'll fancy me when you're drunk.' She tried to laugh, started to cry instead.

She left me to find my own way out. I was crying too. I didn't even like the guy.

I don't feel like getting introspective or analytic, so I run all the way to Gay's place, through the puddles.

It's one of the new shiny-green-brick places with the yellow roof and red paintwork, supposed to be cheerful. Four storeys high, four flats wide, two deep, and the windows are too small. About as cheerful as a gassed-out badger sett. I think they're there as targets for the bombers that buzz over occasionally, distract their eyes from the richies in the city. But don't worry, a bomb hasn't fallen on London for about two years now, and that was one of our guys who flipped his lid. Crazy bastard bombed St Paul's, swore he'd flattened the Kremlin. Went to the firing squad thinking he was a national hero. He was too.

The place has only been up four years and already it's got leprosy. These days you don't have to vandalize the buildings, they do it to themselves.

The door's open so I go on up.

Smells of urine and pine and there are flypapers hanging from the broken hallway lights. A bevy of black and white kids is playing a game on the stairs with what look like dog faeces. I have to clamber over them.

One of the girls looks at me like a whore. She's about nine. I dash on up to the third floor and she looks disappointed. Jesus. She probably only wants to buy a comic.

I pause outside the door to smooth down my hair which duck-bums at the back when it gets wet. I wipe my lips on a sleeve. Gotta look good when you go to meet your honey. Flatten my eyebrows down with a bit of spit.

Me and Gay have been going together for about two years now. I met her at a dance at the Hackney El Dorado, which is where all we cool people go to hang out. No, I tell a lie, it's where all we poor people go to hang out. A sort of ersatz night club. Imitation everything. You can even buy watered-down drinks to make your dough go further and people bring their own records for the disco. Cheap and cheerful? More like cheap and dreadful. It's a place to get drunk in and little more.

I knock on Gay's door, bam bam bam with my knuckles. A voice calls out, but not Gay's. It's Rachel, the flatmate.

'Waddya want?'

'It's me,' I cry. 'The neighbourhood rapist.' I'm a barrel of laughs.

There's a long pause, like the door wants to stay shut. But eventually it opens and Raych invites me in with a jerk of the head. She kind of smiles, or it might be a trick of the light, and I think what the hell's up with her? Raych usually likes me okay. It's very upsetting to a sensitive soul when people are cool.

'She's on the bed.'

'Is she ill?'

Raych shrugs, picks a piece of tobacco from her tongue, looks weary. 'Nah.' She yawns. 'Kind of.' I feel sorry for her, she looks unhappy. But I'm worried. 'What's the matter?'

'She's had a rough time.' She leads me into the bedroom.

Raych is pretty cute. Kind of tallish, slim, heavy in the bosom, with lots of curly brown hair tumbling around her face. Not today though, today it's just greasy, today it just flops. An interesting face, full of ridges and shadows and a taut masculine mouth, blue eyes that are turning grey, a silver loop in her left nostril. She usually wears green eyeshader, negress lipstick. I like her. You wouldn't think she's only nineteen.

I look past her at Gay on the bed. I move past her to Gay on the bed. She's asleep. It looks pretty deep.

I look at Rachel with some fright. 'What is it?'

Rachel peels the ciggy from her bottom lip, blinks as a needle of smoke pricks an eye. 'She's just faded I think. You know. I think it's reaction.'

Sometimes Rachel can be pretty obtuse. 'Reaction to what?'

'The Poh-lice had her for a couple of days. I think she's just wasted.' She leaned past me, pulled back the coverlet to show me Gay's arm. There were four red bruises on the crease of the elbow. 'Looks like she's been narked. She's faded.'

Drugged? What the hell for? I sat down dumbly on the bed edge, filched a fag from Rachel's breast pocket.

She hit me with it while I puffed the fag alight. 'We're hookers. You didn't know did you?'

It was like I'd been slugged with a brick. I went blank.

'She was picked up the other night – they shake us down every now and again. You know they've started that "preventive interrogation" deal at Upminster? Anyway, they have. It's supposed to cut the crime rate, but it won't. I don't know what they want us for anyway, we're not criminals. I don't suppose it does any harm, it just seems a bit stupid. I think Gay must have reacted. They were probably a bit rough, some of them are right bastards.'

Drugs? They use drugs on people like that, with no good reason? Just on the off chance? But 'hookers' overrode it. I felt a bloody fool. I've been going out with a flaming hooker. I couldn't believe it.

'You're upset aren't you?'

Of course I'm upset you stupid bitch. But I couldn't say it, my mouth was as dry as a loofah.

'She didn't want to tell you, but I said she should. I said if you love her, you'll love her whatever. Otherwise it ain't worth it, is it?'

You stupid bitch, you haven't got the faintest bloody idea. I tried to clear my throat. 'How long?' I croaked.

'Who me? Since I was about fourteen. I started –'

No you crazy tart. 'No . . .' I pointed a finger in

49

Gay's direction, stabbed it in the air a couple of times.

'Gay? Not long. Eighteen months maybe. She was saving up so you could go to the States. She was going to surprise you.'

She bloody surprised me all right. I could feel my senses formicating back to me. I could feel myself drawing away.

Rachel rambled on. 'An' of course this place ain't exactly giveaway. Gotta get the spondulicks someplace aintcha? It's the guv'ment's fault really I suppose. I mean, if there was work to do, we'd do it wouldn't we? But they give it all to that other lot. Wouldn't have to go out on wet nights whorin' if they were fair about it.'

She made the word sound so mundane. Christ, it was bloody whoring! It wasn't just something like going to the pub. Jesus Christ. I didn't know what to say. My world wasn't like this.

'She's waking up now look. We've woken her up.'

I jumped from the bed as if there was something contagious in the opening of her eyes.

She looked up at me from the bruises of her eyes, surprised at first, then relaxed. 'Hiya Beak,' she murmured, closed her eyes again on the fringe of sleep.

I didn't answer.

I was all out of things to say. Especially to her.

She looked ill. The urchin face was bruised and shadowy. The always pallid skin was deathly. The cropped green hair was twisted and tacky. Her lips were cold, purple. The eyes were pits.

I stared down at her and I could feel Rachel waiting for me to say something.

'What did you think she was doing?' she screamed at me and I flinched.

Then quite suddenly she slapped me across the cheek. 'What did you fucking expect?'

God, Rachel was so angry with me, tears of rage were shivering in her blue eyes. The slap made my own eyes blur. I put my hand to my cheek.

I stood there in a dumb fog, surrounded by Rachel's sobs and Gay, bewildered and baffled, murmuring sleepily, 'What's up Raych? Whassa matter babe? What's going on?' I couldn't stand it. I stormed out, slammed the door, crashed down the stairs to the smoky street. The kids had set light to another apartment. A ball of smoke hit me in the face.

I looked up and God, the sun was shining. Beaming down on me full of good cheer and jollity. Summer's coming, buck up everybody.

Up your buck sun. I ran off, unconsciously heading for the nearest cheap wine store. My world was falling apart.

FOUR

Well, two days have dragged past and I've arrived at some decisions. Lying on a smelly bed in a grotty tenny with a bottle of cheap hot whisky is a good place to come to decisions.

I was getting the hell out of here. Before anything else went wrong. I mean, a stretch of bad luck's one thing, but when every god in every heaven turns against you, you know you're doing something wrong.

First decision: I've finished with that bloody Gay for good. Like I don't even want to hear her name again. I threw away everything she ever gave me. And a few things she didn't.

How could the bitch treat me like that? How could she be so mendacious?

I don't know. I always thought whores looked like – well, whores. But Gay was so, pretty. Pretty, she was goddamn gorgeous. But like an orchid, she hid a rotten stench. Bitch. I'll never forgive that.

I wonder if she ever really liked me at all? Ah, I can't even talk about it. Let's forget it. She just made use of me.

Second decision: I'm too scared to join the army again, they only want to get me killed. It's their war, not mine, what the hell is Europe to me? What the hell is the other side of London to me come to that?

I'm not going to Woolwich, that's for sure. Which

means of course that I'm obliged to split the scene entirely; they don't just overlook reluctant recruits and move on to something else.

Tomorrow, which is a Monday, I think, I'll mosey on down to the Society in the High Street, take all my dough out. Don't know where I'll go, don't have nearly enough to go anywhere worthwhile. I'll go to the West Country I think. Cornwall maybe, I like the sea. Perhaps I'll get a job on a boat. I don't know, I'll have to decide when I get hold of the money.

Have to bury myself. Deep. Like for ever.

Need a new name too. Something not too interesting, not too memorable. John. Johnny Brady. That'll do.

Third decision: I'm never coming back. Not ever. No contact with anyone, no lonely letters, no furtive phone calls. Finito.

Funny thing really, now I think about it, I seem to have been sloughing the few buddies I ever had in the last year or so. More likely they were just forgetting me. Who wants a miserable bugger like me for a mate? Still, I haven't been shedding any tears so it doesn't bother me. What the hell. They weren't much anyhow.

So that's it, three good decisions. Not bad for a weekend's chugging. I lie here in my own squalor feeling satisfied; it's always good to come to decisions. Feeling boozy.

FIVE

Would you credit it?

Would you screwing believe it?

I could murder someone, I really could.

I get up see, bright and early, about half-past ten.
Had a cold wash. Changed shirts. Brushed my ducks.
Put on my best jacket. All spruced up and somewhere to
go. Trotted out into the springtime air feeling good,
looking cool. Albeit somewhat crapulent.

Clutching my grubby pink account book in my hot
little mitt I trot down to the nearest Society office,
which is about two miles away, and queue up like a
domino for an hour and some, behind a woman
who silent farts and makes out it's not her and a kid
with a green runny nose. But it doesn't matter. I'm
feeling good, I can handle it. Outside the weather's
dandy. I'm a man with a purpose. Fate, don't stop me
now.

But when I finally, like just before the end of the
goddamn world, get there, to the grotty plastic counter
with the spitty plastic screen, this plastic chick with
luminous lips says: 'You've been served an enlistment
order, all your funds have been temporarily frozen.
They'll be released when you produce card PD40.'

'What? Where do I get that?'

'At the Enlistment Office when you report.'

I looked at her as if she'd just told me my wife had

given birth to frogs. It was so patent I couldn't believe it. I was flabbergasted. Over a barrel.

Twelve hundred quid I had, and ten pence. Twelve hundred quid. And they weren't going to let me have a penny.

'Can't I have anything?'

'No.'

Funny how the obvious comes as a complete surprise. I gave her a look that should have sunk a battleship; but she wasn't looking.

I reeled out of the place with all my plans collapsing in temporary freezings about my ears. Thwarted at the first hurdle, nobbled in the feedbox. I was a mug in every direction. What had I done wrong? All of a sudden, everything in the entire world was agin me. What the hell had I done? What had I done?

I looked through both my pockets – a packet of chewy, eleven quid and a paper hanky, with a week to the next welfare payment. What can you do with eleven quid? I blew it on a bottle of gutrot whisky and some shag. Tobacco that is.

The world was ganging up on me. I felt morose. I felt sorry for myself. I felt bloody terrible. I knew this was bound to bring my pimples out again.

SIX

Looked out of the gap in the cobwebs early *ce matin* and there was a rainbow. A rainbow, bending backwards over London.

Rainbows always excite me. Always a puzzle. Nobody can really explain them you know. All that stuff about refraction and water droplets and prismatic effect etc. is so much hooey. I'll tell you something. Rainbows are magic. It's the only explanation that fits. Rainbows are magic. I've given it a lot of thought. Scientists, they don't know everything.

It wasn't a great rainbow but it was a good one.

I lost the last of my whisky when I knocked the flaming bottle over. Which is the kind of thing that never happens to somebody else, always to yourself. Well, I don't know what I'm going to do. I've thought about it so much, I think I've thought myself out. All I know is, I need money to move on. And I can't get any. Where does that leave me? Buggered. That's where that leaves me.

Do you know what they do if you don't report for your service? They put you to work on the Ditch and beat you up three times a day. Until you die from something natural, like a broken spleen or haemorrhaging. Not many guys don't report, with their own underwear. You have to know what you're doing if you elect to go on the scram. You have to be pretty confident. Because they send goons called 'hunters' after you to bring you back. And the goons are not nice people. In fact, they're not nice anything. I bet even their mothers hate them.

I found out later that the goon assigned to run me down was called Rickardson. Ex-Police, ATS, IRA (infilt); a psychology graduate, keep-fit votary, teetotal, faggot, sadist, puts in voluntary unpaid overtime because he enjoys his work. Looks like a statue; by that I mean solid, strong, exaggerated of muscle, cold, deathly, devoid of a heart.

They called him Homer. And not because he reads Latin. Homer. That's what I call him.

Thought you'd just like to know what a goon is like. In case you ever have to run. You have to decide which is worse. The war in Europe or the hunter in the warren. The stoat. The killer. The terror in the darkness.

Was out for a few minutes yesterday, buying a couple of Mars Bars. While I was away a note was slipped under the door. From Gay. It was written on the back of an old Christmas card.

God it tore my guts up. Things like that always do.

The Gables
28 April a.m.

Hi,

I thought I'd better write this note before I set off, in case you aren't in. Sorry about the paper, it's all I can find.

I see the clouds are leaking again. I hope this isn't an omen. Raych has borrowed my coat to go visit her mother. Who is a cow. She's the lump of hair in the bottom of your soup.

I guess I'm not your favourite person hey? Sorry lovely, I would have – no, I don't suppose I would have told you. Not yet. Maybe never. It's something I guess I tried not to think about. I really bawled out poor Raych, though she only did what she thought was best. She was worried about me, I think, so she got angry. She's only young, I guess that's it.

I kept hoping you'd come back so I could – but I knew you wouldn't. (Can you read this cramped writing?) So, it looks like I'm on my way over.

Not to offer excuses. Even hookers have some pride you know. Just to, I don't know, just to tell you. God look at that rain coming down! I hope you're not out in it. I did it to get money. For us. So we could go to America. So we could get married. That's all. There was no way we could get it. No one was going to just give it to us, were they? I'd do anything to get out of this godawful city. Anything, except hurt you Beak. Which is why I wouldn't have told you, but it's all out now anyway.

Please come back. I miss you. We'll make it some other way.

All my love,
Gay

PS I can't wait for ever. If I haven't heard from you in twenty years or so I'll go alone.

PPS I brought you a Mars Bar but I couldn't get it under the thingy, so I ate it.

At first I screwed it up and aimed to throw it in the bucket where I put my clothes to soak. But I missed and then I uncreased it and folded it carefully and put it in my shirt pocket. Goddamn, why do people have to wedge into your life, why can't they just leave you to rot?

Two years we went together. Two years. Goddamn.

*

'Aunt Mel?'

'Um?'

'I need your help.'

'Help?'

'Yes.'

'Yeh?'

Goddamn, it was like talking to a bloody parrot. Why didn't she just stop picking out her teeth for a minute and pay attention? 'Help?' she repeated. 'What sort of help? Is your bike broke again?' Aunt Melanie may not be many things, but a great fixer of bikes she is.

'No,' I said. 'It's not that kind of help I need. It's . . .' I wasn't sure how to begin this.

She twisted on the pouffe that she'd been threatening to explode – she had been teetering over a grey shaving mirror like a god suddenly discovering its reflection in a flat ocean – and nodded me to a chair with a wobble of her dazzling head. 'What is it?' she asked decisively. 'Are you in trouble?'

I perched on the edge. 'Yes. Sort of. I've been called up, for my Beta service.'

'Uhuh. And you don't want to go?'

'Right.'

'Hmm.' She looked thoughtful. 'This isn't an uncommon problem.'

'Uhuh.'

There followed a silence which lasted a couple of minutes. She looked through the window, at the top of the brown building opposite, where against a silvery sky a tiny grey woman was wrestling flapping bedsheets on to a rotary dryer. 'There's no medical reason you can't go?'

'None that I can discover. I need to borrow some money,' I said quickly. 'I have more than a grand in the

Society, but I can't get at it until I've been signed up. I need the money now.'

Aunt Mel lit two ciggies, passed one to me, red with lipstick. (There's always something sexy about that.)

'What I thought. . .' I started to examine my bitten nails. Good God, they were so bitten I could hardly find them. 'I thought perhaps, if you could loan me about five hundred, I'll give you my book, and make out an authorization for you to have the money. I don't see why we couldn't do that. Once I'd gone there wouldn't be. . .' I trickled out. It was a pretty crazy scheme.

Aunt Mel thought about it for a time. 'What do I get out of it?'

'You'd have the money in my account. Twelve hundred quid.'

'Might be years before they let me have that. If they ever did.' She looked me straight in the eye. In a very disturbing fashion. 'I mean, what's in it for me, now?' My heart began to pound nervously.

I don't think I've told you much about myself yet. I'll fill you in a bit.

I was born in Leyton, east London, twenty-six years ago, in a thunderstorm. I shouldn't have been born for a further three weeks, but thunder terrified the shit out of my mother. I'm an August child, all gust and no guts.

I was born at a very inconvenient time, in that my father didn't want a child at all, and he walked out of the house and didn't come back until I was six months old.

My mother was a sickly woman. Sick of my dad, sick of where we lived and pretty soon sick of me. She was one of the world's great 'one-dayers'. But she stayed put and filled with creases at an early age, and looked every inch a defeated woman. Which is what she was.

I didn't help a great deal by virtue of being a very uncooperative child. I wouldn't walk until I was almost two, didn't talk until three, and persisted in wetting the bed until I was twelve. This made my old man intensely angry, which encouraged me to wet the bed even more. As a child psychologist, on a scale of one to ten, my father rated about zero. My childhood, as far as my father was involved, consisted of a series of running battles. He supplied the battles. I ran. I remember that one time, when I was about seven, I hit him back with a lump of brick that I'd found and wanted for a pet. He didn't say anything, but walked out to the kitchen where my mother was, dragged her into the living-room and beat the living daylights out of her, right in front of me. He hit her in the stomach so hard that he punched vomit out of her. I never hit him again.

Fortunately my dad, who was Franklyn's brother John, wasn't always there. He used to spend most of his time wandering around lower London in a methylated fog, shacking up with various desperate and degenerate women. My mother swore at least four times a week that one day she'd kill him. But she never did.

My mother wasn't an attractive woman. She was small, griseous and bony and her hands were incredibly ugly – tiny, purple, rough things like the paws of some inquisitive little creature – I used to dread them touching me, hard and cold and damp they were. Nor was she an affectionate woman. She would hug and cradle me madly for the first couple of days after my dad set off on his binges. But I could never decide whether that was from fear that he might come back, or that he mightn't. We passed most of the time playing cards, or she would read to me from a stock of coverless books kept under her bed; or we would watch the old, haunted telly that sat in the centre of the table like an enormous, frantic family that we weren't a part of. She was a hell of a gin-player my mother. A hell of a cheat too. She should have worked the casinos, she really should. If her hands hadn't been so tiny you would never have known what she was up to.

Funny part was, she used to cheat so that I'd win. It's not funny really, is it? Her name by the way was Louisa, Louisa Annalee Howard, née Harris. They say it's bad luck to marry into the same initial, and my mother confirmed it.

When I was about nine, she won fifteen hundred pounds on one of the lotteries and invested it all in the Society. She had the book made out in my name and it was kept, in a plastic bag, under my sheet. Thanks to the bedwetting that was the last place my dad would look for anything.

He never did find out about that win. Which is probably just as well; he'd have killed us both so that he could claim as next of kin.

I can recall only one display of affection from my old man and that was when he backed a dog called Beak the Streak up at the Stow and it came in at twelve to one. He brought me home a little wire monkey, which could be bent into any shape you liked, ruffled my hair with his stinking hands and gave me three pounds.

I started at Cardinal Allen Primary School on my fifth birthday. My mother was relieved that the school sounded Catholic, even though we were only when-all-else-has-failed Catholics, and I think I was the only one at the place.

I've always sort of liked those 'there when you need

it' religions myself, which is one reason I'm not overly fond of the Roman Church. There are a lot of so-called Romans living around here and the damn drunken priests are always calling round trying to whip up a congregation. They'll never take sod off for an answer. I don't like it when they push on you, seems like private enterprise. I haven't been to church since I was seventeen, when my mother died. And the damn priest was drunk and had his surplice on back to front and got my mother's name all wrong; he kept calling her Margaret Louise, whoever she is. Maybe I was at the wrong funeral.

Schooldays were no great shakes.

I didn't make any real friends there. No one who lasted further than the gates. There was only one guy who impressed me at all, and that was a lad younger than me who could fart at will and masturbate to ejaculation in about fifteen seconds flat. But it didn't do him much good. He died from leukaemia when he was fifteen. There's probably a lesson there somewhere.

Mel stood up with a certain grace and took the two paces across the artificial wolfskin rug that brought her right in front of me, as close and hot and stifling as an electric fire.

As is my custom, I was lost for the next move. But I needn't have worried, one of us at least knew what was going on. Perhaps my ineptness is because I've only ever been with one woman, I don't know. Perhaps I'm simply inherently inept.

I had little time to consider this as Mel put a trembling pair of hands behind my head and slowly pulled my face into the furnace of her belly, swaddling me in the satiny folds, nearly suffocating me. She gave a little high-pitched groan, or was it her stomach gurgling? I'll never know. And she simply held me there for some time, pulsating gently against me. I was conscious of the cigarette still smouldering in my right hand and terrified that I might suffer a sudden rush of passion, lose all control and burn someone. My other hand had perched itself daintily on my knee.

Just before the heat and lack of oxygen made me pass out, Mel relaxed the grip and eased my face away. A zipper running down the front of the housecoat had trapped a hair of my moustache; I squealed as the sudden agony whipped a tear to my eye.

With a quite startling suddenness Mel ripped open the front of the housecoat to reveal a whole world of pink, slightly damp, creased flesh, with a bosky pubic area carefully shaved into the shape of a heart. Worse than that, her massive nipples had been pierced and thin gold loops glinted through them with a chain dangling between.

Regrettably I was ceded only a moment to explore this vision as fierce hands gripped me again, rammed my face into the more than considerable skin of her belly. A reluctant nose ventured into the far reaches of her cavernous navel. She was wet and salty on my lips. Like a plucked gull.

This time I manfully pinched out the cigarette and flicked it away. I put my hands solidly on a pair of momentous buttocks and began to squeeze. As I once watched a master baker.

I realized, as a dense grey murk enveloped me, that Mel was still puffing away madly on her cigarette.

SEVEN

Afternoon, evening, night passed, swimming in the heated pool of Mel's strong arms, and I awoke mid-morning bruised and weak, with a great weight snoring contentedly across me.

I'm not going to tell you what went on during those long, tempestuous hours of unleashed passion, this isn't a peep show. Suffice to say that Mel is an enthusiastic if careless lover and I'm not as fit as I thought.

She cooked me a gargantuan breakfast. It was the first meal I'd had for a day and I was ravenous. I'll say that for Mel, she gives you an appetite. But, as I'd feared, the food was abysmal; on a scale of one to ten it would rate about two. But that's still better than you get in the welfare canteens.

To make me feel more at home she bustled about starkers. But, to be honest, the best that could be said about that is that most of the time she was in another room; it's not a body you'd care to look at too long. Not while you're eating.

About noon I managed to tear myself away. Mel had come over very loving by then, but I needed to get some sleep. I'm not bragging about my prowess, I just don't sleep well in strange beds. I only feel at home in my own home.

Mel promised to loan me the money. I was to come

back for it tomorrow. She kissed me on the outside steps – a searing mercurial kiss that set the neighbours' curtains trembling – and promised me anything I wanted. But I think she meant sexually rather than in terms of a bigger loan. I was somewhat shell-shocked as I shambled home.

Had a strange feeling when I got back that somebody had been in my room. I don't know why, nothing seemed to be out of place, though that doesn't mean a lot because I couldn't remember in what sort of mess I'd left it. But there was a distinct, rather uncomfortable aftertaste. Like somebody else's aftershave on your pillow.

Anyway, nothing was missing so I quickly forgot it. I had other things on my mind. For it had just dawned on me, on the way back from Mel's, as I crossed a stretch of rubble that had once been a nice block of shops and flatlets, just what it was I was doing.

I was hooking. Like Gay.

It didn't make me feel bad, I didn't think, oh Christ how low have I stooped? But I did think, how the hell can I accuse Gay, when I'm doing it myself? If it's good enough for me . . .

A sobering thought. After all, I was the guy she went with for the last two years. So how much could the hooking mean? It couldn't be that she preferred other guys to me, it was just a business. We needed money, she got it the only way she could. When there are thirteen million people unemployed you can't pick and choose.

But later I thought again, is it that simple? For me it's just a one-off, but Gay's been doing it for eighteen months. With lots of men, men she doesn't even know. Filthy, salacious, repugnant men who probably don't even wash. I was pretty confused. I had to think about it.

That's how I spent most of the rest of that day. Reading and rereading that letter from Gay, drinking weak grey tea and giving myself a headache. Mind you, this is the way I usually spend my days, lounging miserably about, listening to the radio, supping dreadfully weak tea from my pint mug.

I began masturbating when I was fourteen and practised hard and regularly because I thought it my best chance of stunting my growth. At that age I was already six feet tall and I wasn't slowing down, which is embarrassing to a sensitive child. I hated being picked on by thugs smaller than myself and I figured this was a chance for them to catch me up. It never occurred to me that they were also probably masturbating away furiously, stunting their own growth.

As you can see, my understanding of matters physical was somewhat warped. I put it down to a negligent and downright poor education. Mind you, if you think I'm bad you should see the rest of them.

School was a disaster; intellectually, socially, on every level. The teachers had come to realize that their purpose wasn't to educate – what for? we couldn't do anything when we left – but to keep us in order until three o'clock. Various methods were tried, the stick, sweet reason, bribes (sexual demonstration in the case of one lovely young teacher called Rebecca, who alas was all too quickly transferred). Anything was worth a try; we ignored them all.

I did master reading and writing – I was fortunate in that books were my mother's sole interest – but I can't do much in the way of rithmetic. What's the point anyway?

I did learn some Russian. *Nyet. Da. Spasibo.* And I know that water is made of H_2O, whatever that is. But that's about all. Most of the lessons I had at school were of the survival-kit type.

It was a pretty bad school, no two ways about it. The worst thing is, it was completely typical. The whole state education system was geared to turning out a generation of imbeciles. Kids in the city with their fancy expensive schools might be pretty bright, but we kids on the other side of the social fence were the darkness which let them shine. Anyway, it eventually became time to leave, and like everyone else I went straight on to Welfare. I was sixteen then, still living at home.

I was very surly. I didn't like being so stupid. Being obtuse suits some people, but I was always bored. The whole bloody world bored me. I just couldn't get into it.

I spent most of the time just sitting at home with my mother, reading boring coverless books. My dad had finally left for good when I was fourteen and I for one didn't miss him at all.

But mother and I didn't speak to each other, we just sat around. There wasn't anything to say. She used to watch the telly a lot, and talk to herself in a kind of pidgin. She wasn't too well really, and died the next year from cancer of the bowel. That was in 2011, the year the Soviets rolled over Belgium and Holland.

I lived quietly on in the tenny for a while and there wasn't really very much difference, except I had to burn my own meals. But the landlord found out eventually and turfed me out.

It was then I tried living in hostels for a few months; but that's not something I'd recommend. I was nearly raped a couple of times.

The army took me in hand for two years, extended it for a third when they found out we might be joining the war, and taught me how to run across the Yorkshire moors with a load of gear on my back, and how to shoot holes in cardboard cutouts of Soviet infantrymen. If this country is ever invaded by a cardboard army I'll know just what to do.

Then I lived with Franklyn for a few months while Aunt Mel was in hospital having mysterious internal things done to her. Which again is not something I'd like to repeat. So I moved into the mildewy slum I now inhabit and hung around for a time with some of the guys from the other rooms. They were a diverse accumulation, blacks, whites, homos, straights, and they didn't mind my sullen reticence. We used to go to clubs and races, parties and things, and although I never grew close to any of them it helped to fill the time while I waited, as all truly idle folk wait, for something to happen.

Two years ago I started dancing with this cute chick at the El Dorado. She's about five-two, popped in a green mini skirt, purple shirt, brilliant copper hair, crossbow eyes.

I'd seen her there before, but as the type who never seemed short of partners. So I stayed a wistful watcher in the wings. I'm not the pushy sort, I have to be pretty certain before I'll sidle up to anyone and mumble something incoherent about tripping the light fantastic. I always wound up with dumpy little girls with enormous thighs, with big bovine eyes that never leave you, terrified you might split in the dance and leave them stranded. They never said much, but hung on every dumb word that was maundered and grinned a lot. We were a pretty pathetic crowd. Except for the chick in the green mini. She had class.

EIGHT

Somebody was watching me when I left the building this morning. I'm sure of it.

Why should he do that?

It was about eleven, I needed some groceries. If it had been raining I'd probably have managed without, but it was a frisky day, warm and golden, so I crawled out of the blanket and blundered into my livery. Smoothed down my hair with a smear of margarine and was ready to go.

A shave would have been in order – my stubble starts to curl and prick my chin when it's so long – but I couldn't face all the blood. I thought I looked a bit haggard, pale too, my eyes were red. I looked like a ghoul. But I wasn't posing for any pictures so I told the ego not to worry.

For the record, I had on my faded straight black cords, my holey pink and fawn Levi boots, a black knitted shirt and my khaki canvas jacket with the stains. I'd parted my lank hair on the left and it clung like an oil slick, a spiky fringe coiling rather stupidly into my right eye. My moustache was looking pretty pancho, but the sparse bearding underneath looked like a nylon broom frizzled by a match. I had a steel loop through my left ear, and at the back my hair was beginning to stick out over my collar.

This is my punko-bohemian look, a style not imitated

the whole world over. It's kind of old-fashioned. These days the trend is for baggy bright clothes and long wavy hair. Me, I'm a diehard. Also, I can't afford it.

I tripped down the steps in my famous slouch, a red shopping bag slung jauntily over the right shoulder.

Half a newspaper was aping a wounded bird at the bottom of the steps and it was as I hoicked it up to have a look that I realized I was being watched. From a hooded doorway across the divoted street, somebody suspiciously ordinary was looking at Barty Kafka Howard.

Now it's odd I should think that, for the nondescript character who slouched there wasn't even looking in my direction, he was staring up the street to where some kids had stacked a bonfire. But I sensed that it was for me the little man's attention was reserved. He appeared suspiciously unoccupied. And an apprehensive cloud accumulated over me like the skin on a cup of coffee.

I wasn't scared, exactly. Certainly wary, but after all he was only a little hombre. I figured if he turned out to be a faggot or a mugger I could probably handle him. But his surreptitious surveillance was discomfiting, as if someone had set a balance to swinging, and I was in one of the pans.

I spectated him carefully for a few moments, while simulating a scan through the paper; but not once did his steady gaze swivel by a flicker in my direction. Nothing suggested he was even aware of me. Maybe I was wrong. Perhaps it's just my paranoia

No clue could be gleaned from his appearance. He was the sort of bozo you see in any crowd, shabby, tired, sullen, preoccupied. If you took your gaze away you wouldn't remember him.

I stuffed the paper into the bag and headed for the supermarket. Then at the top of the street, beyond the crackling fire and the screaming kids, I whirled and looked back – maybe I glimpsed him through the swirling smoke and burning paper birds, maybe not.

I continued uneasily, reluctant to glance behind again. Something nascent yet familiar seemed to be haunting me, treading in my troubled footprints. I couldn't put a finger on it, and I wasn't sure I wanted to. I hate mysteries.

Early evening I set off for Mel's, hoping she'd give me some tea. The gas in our block was off again.

All the way there I had to keep peeking anxiously back in case something was padding behind me. But there was nothing. I came to the conclusion that I must have been mistaken about El Nondescripto. But like all of my conclusions, it was pretty indecisive.

Mel had really gone to town. The pong when she opened the door nearly wafted me back down the corridor; eau de something cheap but strong, it probably took stains out of wood as well.

She was dolled up like a novice queer, flawless make-up, impeccable hair, clingy turquoise blouse, tight leather skirt, high black patent boots, moist lipstick. My heart sank as soon as I saw her and my first thought was: I'm not going to get the money. Cynics always have first thoughts like that.

The germ was knocked out of me as a kiss that reached right down to my groin and tied my ears in knots smothered me.

We were panting heavily when Mel finally unpeeled, partly from passion, but mainly asphyxiation I think.

She grabbed me by a hand, led me into the living-room. Oh God, the table was all laid, serviettes, wine, twisted red candles, the lot. I thought: I'm in the wrong play, this isn't my scene – but already Mel had pressed me into a chair, sucked the breath out of me with another of her boiler-room kisses. I hadn't even had a chance to say hello yet.

She lit me a cigarette, slopped out a tumbler of whisky, poured into the kitchen like a vase on a potter's wheel. So I sat there alone, feeling like a prick, twiddling with my tumbler. This wasn't exactly what I'd expected. I don't really understand people at all, you know.

The whisky caught in my throat and made my eyes water.

'Did you get to the Society?' I mumbled awkwardly as she passed through the room.

Mel lit a cigarette, didn't look at me. 'Uhuh. They said I couldn't have that much on demand, I'll have to go back in a week.'

'A week?' Jesus Christ.

'So they said.' She prised the moistened cigarette from her lower lip, left a shred of paper dandruff there. 'I was thinking. Why don't you stay here for the week, you could . . .'

My spirits slumped like a lump of mashed potato. She was playing me along. I was being eased into Franklyn's shoes. I'm not that stupid.

NINE

Today I went to see Gay. But she was not there. She is in gaol. I couldn't believe it.

The door was on the latch. When I went in Rachel was sprawled on the sofa asleep, her arms flung out. She looked awful. She'd been knocked about and she'd been crying. Her hair was all over the place, her jet eyeshader was smudged into big panda markings, her lip was swollen right up, and the ridge of her left cheek was purpling. The backs of her hands looked as if they'd been scratched, pustules of dried blood stood up on the knuckles, and it looked as if someone had kicked her right ankle, there was a huge pink lump showing just below her jeans.

'Rachel? Rachel – are you all right?'

The panda eyes opened and two enormous tears peered unhappily out at me.

'Beak?' She blinked the tears out of the corners of her eyes, wiped them off her cheeks with the back of a hand. She had a good sniff. 'Is that you Beak?'

'Yeah. It's me, Raych.' I was really upset, I've never seen a girl in a state like that, I wanted to cry. I knelt down, cupped the least damaged hand in both my own. 'What happened, Raych? Are you okay?'

She tried to shrug it off. 'Yeah, sure. Takes more than a few knocks to keep me down.' But she didn't mean it and she put her free hand up to her face as a fresh spate of tears came. 'Bastards,' she whimpered. 'Bloody bastards.'

I cradled her in my arms, she buried her face in my shoulder, bawled into my jacket. I just held her like that for a couple of minutes, trying to keep my own tears down. God, it's terrible when a woman cries. She was really streaming; lots of women go through the motions of crying, but this was a real damburst. She was squeezing on the back of my neck like a little girl.

When finally she eased away Rachel looked desolate. She rubbed and snuffled her nose all over her face, trying to sort herself out. Then she continued gulping huge convulsive sobs, almost as though she was about to be sick, and her eyes were wandering all over the place, drunk between the glistening pikestaffs of her lashes. Her nose was running so I gave her my hanky to blow on. Thank God it was clean.

'Good ol' Beak,' she mumbled. 'Always there with a clean hanky.' She mapped it out with smears of mascara and lipstick. 'I said you'd be back.'

'What happened, Rachel? Who did this to you?' She didn't seem to hear me.

'Who was it, do you know?'

She sniffed, nodded once, tightly. 'Yeah.'

'Who?'

'Fitzwilliam. James Fitzwilliam.'

The name meant nothing.

'He came for Gay.'

'Gay?'

Rachel sniffed. 'Yeah. He had a thing about her. She's been trying to get rid of him for months, but he kept turning up again.'

'Here?' I asked numbly. 'She used to bring him here?'

'No,' said Rachel. 'We never brought anyone here, except genuine boyfriends. But he found out, he turned up here tonight with one of his shadows.'

76

'What happened?'

'He tried the charm first. Bottle of whisky, big chummy smiles. Then when Gay started losing cool he turned nasty, started slapping out at both of us.' She blew her nose like a foghorn. 'Then Gay stabbed him in the shoulder with the bread knife.'

'She what?'

'Well she was frightened, we both were. He's a big guy and unpleasant with it.'

I lit my last trembling cigarette, swapped puffs with Rachel. 'Then what happened?'

'They took her away in the van and he went off to hospital.'

'Where did they take her?'

'The Green I suppose. Fitzwilliam's the Chief Inspector there.'

'He's a bloody flic?'

'Yeah, a lot of the clients were. Guys like you can't usually afford us.' She grinned cheekily.

Rachel passed me the cigarette. 'She hadn't been with anyone since that night you came around. She'd finished the business, she only did it for your boat fare.'

My thoughts were in a whirlpool, sucked down a confused vortex to where nothing appeared straightforward. 'How badly hurt was this Fitzwilliam?'

Rachel shrugged. 'It made him faint. But I don't think he was too bad, else he wouldn't have been so angry.'

'What do you think they'll do with her?' I passed the cigarette again.

'I don't suppose they'll give her a medal. She'll probably go to court tomorrow, and then . . .' her voice faded into ether.

My throat tightened. 'And then what?'

TEN

I had visitors this morning, early.

I thought the tapping was someone chiselling a coffin, but it was the tail of a bad dream, and when I realized what was actually going on whoever was at the door was practically thumping it off the hinges.

I stumbled out of the quicksand blankets. 'Yeh wassabloodymarrer?' I shouted. 'We're norronfire are we?' It takes me a while to get it together when I first wake up. I heard the factory siren howling its head off as I kicked off the bedclothes. Nine o'clock. Good God, it's the middle of the night!

I yanked open the door. 'Hello,' impatiently.

I woke up quickly when I saw the two bozos standing there; one was very short and nondescript, the other was one of the Cairngorms. They didn't look like they'd come to read the meter.

'Are you Howard?' said the little one in a Mickey Rooney voice. I nodded. 'Mind if we come in?'

'Er . . .' Too late, they were in. And me standing there like a prune in my underpants.

They picked their way through all the clutter and sat down on the edge of my bed. The little one reached up and unhooked a pink bra from the green plastic lampshade. 'Is this yours?'

I shook my head. 'My mother's staying with me.' Actually Rachel, frightened that Fitzwilliam's buddy might be back, had moved in with me for a while. This is why I'm sleeping in a pile of quicksand on the floor.

'Where is she?'

Fortunately she was out at the moment, that is to say, she hadn't come in from work yet. 'She's gone to the crematorium.'

The bra was laid neatly on the bed. 'You needn't be so nervous,' said Mickey.

'It's okay,' I squeaked. 'I like being nervous, I'm used to it.'

The Cairngorm stabbed half an inch of cigarette between its green teeth and struck a match on my wall.

'Sit down,' said Mickey.

'Thanks.' I sat down on the pile of blankets as if bones had been removed from my legs.

'You can call me Tommy,' said Mickey. I knew I'd heard that accent before, it was Irish. 'And this is Moose.'

Tommy is the guy I thought was spying from across the street. He looked even smaller now, with a rough, mature head on a young boy's body. A dingy fawn raincoat wrapped around his striped, collarless shirt, blue braces clung on by a fingertip to baggy grey ducks. He had a pair of odd shoes on, one brogue, one Oxford.

Tommy's hungry face was a tight, pinched white frame into which the features had been punched by machine; tiny black eyes like devils, a thin nose, surely too tight to admit sufficient breath, a grey mouth that might snap shut on flies. He needed a shave all round, but his black hair was short and flat enough. He had restless eyes like a squirrel.

Moose, on the other hand, had been tossed pink, lumpy amorphous features; lobeless ears which stuck out like stabilizers, a nose like a circular bath sponge, eyes that were almost hidden below greasy, overweight lids. His eyebrows were virtually non-existent, thin ginger arches quizzical above milky slits that were permanently vacant. His mousey hair appeared to have always been thin and thinning, put there merely as a matrix for the huge flakes of dandruff.

He grinned occasionally, quite without cause or reason, and I'm inclined to believe unconsciously. He was huge though, his clothes must have been castaway sails. Pray God he doesn't collapse on me as I cower here on my little island.

'Sure, it's a shitey place you have here,' said Tommy in a friendly enough way. 'It's a wonder your mother can stand it.'

'I er . . .' What could I say? It's difficult to match that kind of frankness.

'Still, it's better than a bunker or a foxhole, eh? Sure, 'tis a damn sight better than the poison purple gas writhing in and out your dead teeth.' He certainly had a way with words. He pulled one of my old socks from under his buttocks and dropped it pointedly to one side. Moose kissed furiously on his butt, like a dying pipe-smoker.

My gaze flickered from one to the other, flashing them all my fear. I could only think that as I didn't know them, and they'd forced into my room, they intended hurting me. Why, I had no idea.

Tommy scratched an ankle. 'I hear you've been called up.'

'Are you with the army?'

'Ha huh hur!' They both laughed, unpleasantly; a pink plate over Tommy's upper gum slipped down alarmingly. 'No bejaze we're not with the army.' Tommy wheezed, coughed, hawked daintily into a handkerchief. One of mine.

The laughter subsided to a silent prelude. Tommy's Irish eyes bored into me. 'D'yez want to go?'

'Go?'

'Into the army.'

'Er . . .' What was I supposed to say?

'Let me phrase it another way for yez. If you had a chance t'avoid your service – would yez be interested?'

'I don't know,' I stammered. 'It depends on the alternative.'

'Well, let's supposin' there was an organization that wanted to help little boys who didn't want to play soldiers. Supposin' they could get yez out the country, as a favour, for a favour – would yerself be at all interested? Assumin' such a concern existed.'

'I, er – what sort of favour would something like that involve?'

Tommy grimaced. 'Ach, nothin' much. Just a favour. A favour for a favour that's all.'

'Why –'

'Course if you like the British army, then you've no more to be troubled. However,' he stood up with Moose, 'if you'd maybe be interested in hearing some more, me and Moose'll be in the Green Goblin tomorrow night. We'll maybe see you there. Eh?'

I scrambled to my feet but didn't speak, I didn't know what to say.

'Just ask for Tommy. Sure, an' give me best to your ol' mother. Tell her she wears a lovely bra. Toodle-oo boyo, toodle-oo now.'

And without a sign or word from the suspiciously psychopathoid Moose they went out, and left me trembling.

IRA? Seemed like it. But could be anyone. UDA maybe. I searched all over the place for a crushed

cigarette, dragged the smoke in ravenously. How did
they know I'd been called up? Maybe they were with
the security forces? The police? Nah, what'd be the
point?

What did they want me to do?

I was still trembling in my underpants when Rachel
came home half an hour later. 'What's the matter with
you?' she asked as she slumped in on a cloud of perfume.

'Er, nothing. Couple of guys were here, I was just
thinking over what they said. Did you have a good
night?'

She flopped on the bed. 'Nix. Spent most of it in the
Alhambra drinking coffee. Might as well have been
home in bed. You want some breakfast?'

'Yeah. I'll make you some, what do you want,
toast?'

'Fab.' She fell back on the quilt like a discarded dress.
'Jeez my legs ache.'

Later in the day I went down to Leyton Green nick.

The place was crowded, like everywhere. I waited
an hour just to get in the door.

Eventually I got the attention of a spotty young dick
whose uniform was crusty and speckled from people
breathing and coughing on him the day long. His
fingernails had been gnawed right back to the wrists,
his dead blue eyes were all gunged up at the corners.

He was trying to sharpen a yellow pencil by picking
away the wood with his teeth. I had to shout to be heard
above the din. Then I had to poke the dick to call his
attention, so engrossed was he in his beavering.

'I'm trying to find what happened to a friend of
mine!'

Dead-eyes looked up, his tongue grey with graphite. 'You what?' he bellowed.

'A friend! I'm looking for a friend who was brought in here, day before yesterday!'

'Who?'

'Gay Deveraux!'

'Who?'

I was being crushed over the counter by a lot of jostling behind me. A wagonload of drunks seemed to have arrived. 'She stabbed someone, in self defence!'

Dead-eyes sighed, snapped the pencil in two and threw the bits to the floor. 'Deveraux?' He looked in a grubby book. 'Oh yeah, Fitzwilliam's chick.' He laughed. 'I remember.'

Like a stab of lightning in the thunder of my brain I thought: she is not Fitzwilliam's chick, she is my chick. My chick. And I want her back. 'Where is she now?'

'She'll have gone to court today! They went a couple of hours ago!'

'Where?'

'Walthamstow! Can you see any pencils on the floor over there?'

I looked at the mess of legs trampling back and forth across the curling scraps of grey linoleum. It was like a barn dance. 'Can't see one!'

'The bastards keep nicking them!'

I nodded, I was already trying to force a way out. A brawl had flared up and I had to barge backwards through the fringes of it. A woman punched me in the balls.

And when I got outside, I discovered that someone had pinched the Mars Bar out of my pocket. Christ, I ask you.

ELEVEN

Ce soir I journeyed to the Green Goblin pub. It's a mile from the tenny, Stratford way. I arrived about eight, just as the place was beginning to fill, the hour of transition, the dawn of the night. The world is a cupboard and now the dusty toys were creeping out by way of the heavy brown doors with the big brass handles and the axe marks.

I walked slowly through the bar, scanning faces, searching for the cryptic Tommy, the atavistic Moose.

Faces in bars always look the same; it's an observable fact that the same people visit every pub you visit, on the same night, times without end.

This means, in vague theological terms, that you carry the universe around with you; not within your head, as some erudite idiots claim, but on invisible strings in front of your eyes. The eyes are the windows on to the universe, for the god who lurks in the numberless room. Is he a good god, or a wicked god? I don't know, I'm too busy looking for Tommy.

Well, I see all sorts. Old whores with LOVE and HATE and ACAB tattooed across their knuckles, pretty young things who smoke like beginners with their elegant ciggies pointing to Aldebaran, too busy flicking off ash to inhale. I see conspiratorial grey men in worn-down shoes muttering over empty glasses, people who sit alone with tics. I see rustling newspapers drinking halves, girls on dates drinking fancy concoctions they don't even like. I see the true drinkers recognizable by the size of their throats and their squashed legs; and the sippers, who are there because they have nothing else to do.

But I do not see Tommy. Nor do I see the bulwark Moose, who should be as easy to spot as a bride at a funeral.

Three times I stalk around the crimson, horseshoe bar, like a prick, a stranger. Third time I get suspicious looks, so buy a jar of soapy bitter and sup it slowly, leaning casually on the swimming counter, with my back to the bar to show I'm not nosing anybody. I light a ciggy from a smouldering butt in the ashtray. I exhale coolly, trying to look hard. I try to blow a smoke ring; I give up.

This kind of thing goes on for some time. It gets to nine-thirty, I'm feeling a little woozy and still Tommy hasn't shown.

Finally I lean over the bar and command the landlord's attention with an unfortunate belch. 'Excuse me, I'm looking for a guy called Tommy. Little guy, with a bull called Moose.'

The landlord is more interested in taking money than talking to runts like me. He didn't bother looking up as he said, shortly, 'He'll be in.' I slumped back on to my heels, swilled the detritus in the bottom of the glass, lit another ciggy. My twelfth today; I can't afford this kind of extravagance.

Finally, around a quarter past ten, when I'm wondering whether to pass out, throw up or go home (I don't drink so well on my own) Tommy slips in. I see him first at the far end of the horseshoe, joking with some shifty tykes; I blink, and he's halfway round,

85

beetling my way. I daren't blink again in case he walks into me.

'Hello boyo,' he purrs as he slides up to me. 'And what might you be drinkin'?'

'Anything you like,' I say fairly merrily. 'It's all the same to me.' He ordered two Guinnesses. The one drink I cannot stand, but I start on it nobly.

'You've been waiting long?'

'Only this evening.'

'Ah good, good. You'll have thought about me offer then?'

'I have.'

The glittering, vulpine eyes watched me, darkly. 'And?'

'I'm nervous.'

'Nervous? Of me?'

'Erm, partly.' You I don't mind, it's bloody Moose I'm worried about. 'I don't think anyone's going to help me for nothing. What is it I'd have to do?'

'Depends boy. Depends on what is needed, so you might say.'

'But it wouldn't be cheap, would it?'

'No. It wouldn't be cheap.' We quietly quaffed a draught from our frothy glasses.

'It'd be something big then?' I said gruffly, letting the alcohol lend me bravado.

'Big? Well, that depends what you mean by big, doesn't it?'

'Murder,' I said quickly, hoping I was wrong. Please let me be wrong.

'That's big all right,' Tommy agreed. 'Aye, that's big.'

'I don't think . . .' I took a deep breath. 'I don't think I could murder anyone.'

'Well, you might not have to cully might you?' said Tommy cheerily. 'You might not have to.'

'I'll have to think about it.'

'That's understandable. You don't want to be reckless.'

'No.' We finished our pints. 'There is another thing.'

'What's that, cully?'

'There's a friend, I have to take with me. A girl.'

'Ah.'

'I couldn't leave without her.'

'She's your sweetheart then?'

'Kind of.'

'Aha.'

'Does it make a difference?'

'Well, one is one, and two is two, boy. Stands to reason, don't it? You can't have two for the price of one.'

'That's what I thought. So it would be two "favours" then?'

'Two. Aye.'

'But, I could do them both, without her being involved?'

'You could. Have you got a smoke boy, I left mine in me other coat?' I shook one out, lit it for him from my butt.

'Where could we go?'

'Go? Anywhere you like. America?'

America. It was like a shining light. 'America,' I repeated stupidly.

'But you'll be needing time to think about it. You'll need to work it out, in your head I mean.' I nodded. 'When are yez due to go?'

'In four days. On the tenth.'

'Four days ye say, what'd that be, a Friday?' I

nodded. 'Look, I'll tell you what, you have a think about it, and if you decide you don't want to go, meet me in the Black Dog. And bring your things.'

'My things?'

'Sure your clothes and all. You can't go back home you know. We'll fix yez up with someplace to stay. What d'you say?'

'Yeh. I guess so.'

'Sure, well I'll maybe be seeing yez again. But I'll be away now hey, I've gotta buy a racing dog.'

I caught his arm. 'Are you with the IRA?' I asked bluntly.

'The IRA? Sure, and who are they when they're at home?' He grinned and I felt foolish; foolish for asking, foolish for still not knowing. 'Think on this, cully,' said Tommy just before he turned away. 'If you join the British army and they tell you to kill someone, what'll you call that? Would you call that murder?'

Then he was gone, departing as swiftly as he came with that Irish nimbleness. And I was left alone, feeling sick and wondering why the pub was swaying.

I hadn't got anything sorted out; I'd hoped I would. I was still in the dark, ignorant of my own immediate future. God, I hate crossroads. I never know which way to turn. Turn left at every junction, that's how you're supposed to get to the heart of a maze. Always keep to the left.

But which way is left? And which is right?

BOOK TWO

ONE

I thought 2c Arlington House was bad; compared to this old bun it's a bloody wedding cake. They'd better be right about the crock of gold, because this rainbow I'm crossing is a bloody misery.

Do I sound fed up? I am. Here's the rundown.

Inevitably, I turned up at the Black Dog that Friday night. I had all my belongings in two plastic carriers roped to the back of my bike. And times being what they are, I wheeled the whole lot into the bar with me.

This was an Irish pub, full of Shamuses, bejasuses and Holy Marys; gallons of whiskey and black and tan were disappearing down the throats of the crowd, and it was packed, I could hardly get my bike to the bar.

'Sure but that's a pitifully thin girl you've got there,' quipped one Irish wag just before someone hit him over the head with a brown bottle.

I ordered a bitter, looked for Tommy's face in the boozy tumult, feeling conspicuous but exhilarated now that I had actually made my move. I couldn't see Tommy, or Moose, or anyone familiar. I settled down to wait, trying to quell my trembling nerves with the quivering glass of ale.

Rachel was going to stay on in the flat. I'd helped her move her gear over yesterday, and we'd taken all of Gay's stuff to her brother's place in Chingford, very up-market. The landlord wouldn't mind the switch; so long as he got his money he wouldn't care if a pack of rabid dogs moved in. I promised to get in touch when I could.

Gay was sentenced to twenty months with labour. Attached to the Canal project. This, though you might find it difficult to believe, was a real break. We'd thought she would get hard labour; that's working on the Ditch itself. All Gay has to do is make sails for fourteen hours a day.

In case you don't know, the Canal is the brainchild of Winston Cooper, our glorious Home Secretary. It was begun two years ago and should be completed in another three. Its main purpose seems to be to kill people.

To put you in the picture, the Canal will run from Glasgow, Leeds and Liverpool to London, converging at Birmingham. It will be one hundred feet wide, fifteen deep, and WILL BE EXCAVATED BY HAND, BY HUMAN LABOUR. Forced labour. Can you believe that? Through hills of rock, over rivers, motorways, straight through towns – and every gruelling inch hacked out by hand. It's a hell of an idea, you have to admit.

So these days, if you fall foul of the multitudinous laws that were recently drawn up into a ten-volume concise form designed to make them easily accessible and comprehensible to your average plebeian (that's a joke, most of we plebs can't even read) you may find yourself not incarcerated in some gloomy nick, but assigned to a Canal workparty. Brother, rather you than me.

They work you fourteen hours a day. You sleep in what you've dug out that day, rain or shine, or snow, or ice, in a prison sleeping bag. You are encouraged to work hard by overseers equipped with whips, clubs and guns.

If you try to escape, they shoot you.

Many men and women die. Others leave at the end of their term crippled for life. The unlucky ones survive to keep working, fourteen hours a day, seven days a week. A lot commit suicide. Hanging by wire noose is the commonest method.

This is a hell of a government we've got.

The aim of the Canal is to transport Britain's produce up and down and around the country cheaply on sail barges. Which no doubt will be hauled by men when the wind drops. Men, the solution to the energy crisis. Man, the human workhorse.

So you see, in being assigned to the sail factory at Leighton Buzzard, Gay was lucky. She'd probably just wind up with crippled hands.

(It's my belief that when the Canal is finished, it will be filled in and begun again. For ever.)

But on with the narrative. I'd waited in the Black Dog until closing time before Tommy appeared with Moose, who sported a bright yellow sweatshirt with the logo I EAT MY DUCKS RAW in red, dripping letters.

There were no pleasantries. Tommy said, 'Right cully, let's away then.' And led the way. Moose glared at me like I was a duck. Thank God I'm on their side.

We left the pub, turned north, under the railway, through the lampless darkness of terraced London for half a mile. I don't know this area at all, though it's just a couple of miles from my old flat. It looked rough, the sort of district where footsteps echo and unlit buildings watch you.

At length we entered a small empty warehouse,

clanging in to scare the shit out of a few roosting birds. I switched on my bicycle lamp and its timid, frosty glow spilled reluctantly ahead. We proceeded to the farthest corner from the inoperative sliding doors.

I don't know what used to be housed here, the place had been well cleared out. There's nothing here now but a few plastic rubbish bags, heaps of brick and polythene and two holed dustbins. The concrete floor is thick with muck and dust.

At the rear a flight of rickety wooden stairs ascends to a couple of shanty offices. One reeked of lavatories and was littered with mags and news-sheets. It was empty. The other was locked. Tommy opened it, handed me the key. This was my room.

Moose lit a calor gas lamp – I hadn't realized he was that bright. The power to the place had long been cut off. From the musty, urinal smell I think the air had been cut off too. Tommy tried to throw the window open, but it wouldn't budge. 'Never mind,' he said. He didn't have to live here.

'What do I do now?' I asked glumly.

'Make yerself at home,' said Tommy. 'There's beer and grub in the cupboard, water at the end of the yard. We'll come an' see yez in a few days, when we get something sorted out. You just take it easy, lie low. We'll take care of you cully, don't you worry.'

'Do I just wait?' I asked helplessly.

'You're in no rush are you? It's better than Woolwich Barracks.'

I suppose he was right about that. All the same, it's a bit dismal. And lonely.

'You can keep your bike under the bed,' said Moose, doubtless trying to cheer me up.

I nodded. 'It'll like it under there.'

'Come on then Moose,' said Tommy. 'Don't fret cully, tis just for a little while.' He gave me a pack of cigarettes. 'Here's some smokes.'

I followed them out of the door. 'What about a toilet?'

Tommy waved his arms. 'It's a big warehouse. Spread it around, that way it won't smell. So long, cully.' And they trotted into the night, murmuring. I closed and locked the door. I looked around miserably. That was a fortnight ago.

I met Rachel this evening at the Alhambra.

She said, 'A friend of yours called round this morning.'

'Who's that?' I asked, puzzled.

'Homer.'

'Who?'

'Homer. He said his name's Homer. A big geezer, with silver hair.'

'Silver hair?'

'You know, very short and white, so it looks silver.'

'I've never heard of him.' I shook my head, confused.

'He said, "Is Bartholomew Howard in? I'm a friend of his."'

'Doesn't mean anything. What does he look like?'

'Like a ghost. He's got red eyes.'

'An albino?'

'I suppose so. I didn't like him very much. Big bozo though, must have been nearly seven feet high, taller than you. Got a lot of white scars around his jaw, like his chin's been stitched back on. And sticky-out ears.'

'What was he wearing?'

'Just ordinary. Jeans. A jacket.'

'He didn't say he's from the army?'

'No, I'd have told you Beak wouldn't I? I'm on your side remember.'

'I wonder what he wanted.'

'He wanted you.'

'Didn't he say anything else?'

'Nix. I said you'd moved and he just turned round and went. He said, if I see you, tell you Homer called. He doesn't look like one of the good guys Beak. If you see him coming I think you'd better run. Where are you staying?'

'Not too far. If I don't tell you, you can't get into trouble. How are you doing?'

'Okay I guess. Trade's a bit slack. I miss Gay. I get on okay with one of the guys in the other flats.'

'Who's that?'

'Danny. From downstairs.'

'Danny? The homo?'

She laughed. 'He might be a homo to you, he's all right with me. We're kinda going out at the moment.'

'He's all right Danny. The only one of them I ever really liked.'

'Yeah, I like him.'

'I've got to split now Raych. I'm waiting for news, don't like to be away too long.'

She held her lips to be kissed and squeezed my hand. 'Take care Beak, hey?'

I smiled, kissed her again. 'And you Raych. I'll be in touch soon.'

TWO

Apart from the bed – it seemed clean enough but I put my own sheet on to be sure – and the small plyboard cupboard stocked with a few tins and packets of food and a dozen cans of Guinness, the room possesses a few scraps of musty matting, a little calor gas stove, a pan, a mirror, a pile of old newspapers and porno mags, a galvanized bucket which I fill with dodgy water from a tap in the yard, and a small window that looks out on to a corrugated iron roof and a lifeless landscape of rooftops and chimneystacks that rolls on and on for ever.

I think you could pass your life in the room and not see anyone; you could believe you were a prisoner of the pigeons who clatter past from time to time on frantic business.

A few days after I arrived a guy came to replenish the cupboard and load me up with fags. He was a new face, not sure whether to be surly or friendly.

He is young, with a monk's hair and a wispy beard. His name is Harry. He's Irish too. Moose isn't. He's from the northeast I'd say.

I hope something happens soon, I'm lonely. To tell you the truth, I get the willies.

The nights are the worst. I hear noises. And I'm not a brave man.

THREE

Harry came again this morning. He gave me an address and a street map; I'm to be somewhere at three tomorrow.

Just as well he came today, the batteries in my radio are about shot; much longer and I'd never know the time.

Pity he didn't stay. I would have liked someone to talk to.

Today I counted all the rooftops.

FOUR

This morning I am afraid.

Not a fanciful passing fright, nervousness which will
dissipate when I get underway. I have real fear deep in
my guts, churning me up; dread that commands my
thought, that tries to disguise itself in attacks of nausea.
But it's like a cuckoo passing off as a nestling
wren. Only a wren couldn't tell the difference, and
I'm no wren. I'm a sitting duck. I'm scared, really
scared.

Do I exaggerate? I'll tell you why I'm sore afraid.

This morning I awoke as usual, bleary and muggy,
coughing to warn the world of my arrival. Turned over
to get a ciggy, saw something.

On the bed, just below my chin, was a small white
card. A calling card. Puzzled, I picked it up and zoomed
it into focus. It was handwritten, not neatly, in blue ink.
And its message was clear enough: 'I'll be back
Howard'. and signed 'Homer'.

My hand began to tremble. I snapped up as if I'd been
electrocuted, looked to the door as a condemned man
might look to the door of his cell when he hears the final
rites approaching. It was closed. I always lock the door,
even if I just nip out for a slash I lock it behind me. The
window too was closed.

I sprang out of bed, clad in my best pair of blue
underpants. I yanked on the doorknob. The door was

open! It had been unlocked! I gave a little squeak as it swung back in my hand.

As soon as I realized it was opening I expected to see some ghoul standing there about to strike me dead. Or a god. Perhaps the god Homer, who opens locks and tracks down the well hid. Who is arrogant and sure, who announces his coming in the manner of those who are never thwarted, the invincible, who see through walls, who knows all of London, every house, every room, every tiny frightened person. Who the hell is he? What does he want with me?

I slammed the door and locked it, cringed back against the farther wall. I rushed to the window. Nothing. Nobody in sight. Just a pigeon.

What does he want with me? He must be army. Mustn't he? What if it's something to do with the trip with Franklyn. Maybe he's just some pervert, plenty of them around. It doesn't seem very military to sneak into people's rooms like that, surely they'd just arrest you? Why why why? I rushed back to the door, barricaded it with the bed, the cupboard, everything.

Then I sat on the edge of the bed and struggled into my clothes.

With a dreadful chill infiltrating my veins I thought, when will he be back? An hour, tonight, tomorrow, a week? Right now? Should I wait here? Should I run?

But run where, I've nowhere to go. And perhaps he's waiting downstairs, in the gloom of the warehouse. Perhaps he's leaning against a metal strut, chewing a chocolate bar, staring at my door, waiting. I needed to go to the toilet.

I peed out of the window. But it wasn't enough. My bowels wanted a go too.

I couldn't go outside though. Finally I tipped the last

of the water into the saucepan and used the bucket. God, what a mess I was in. All of a sudden I'm falling apart at the seams.

I kept having convulsions, shuddering as if I was freezing. I'm one of the world's true cowards.

I dismantled the bed, smashed a piece of wood a couple of feet long out of it. It was better than no weapon at all; and whatever Homer wanted, it wasn't going to be good. Like I don't do the football pools.

I clutched the club fervently as I sat on the floor and stared at the door.

An age passed. I suddenly remembered my appointment and jumped up to put the radio on. It was one-thirty. I needed to give myself an hour to find the place. I ought to be going, I'd be safer on the street.

I looked out of the window again. But I didn't fancy the drop down to that rusty corrugated roof a dozen feet below. I turned back and carefully began to remove the barricade from the door, piece by piece, as slowly and quietly as I could.

When just the door remained I started trembling again, not a gentle quivering, this was a real shaking, head to toe stuff. I stared at the knob for ages, convinced it was about to turn.

I turned the key. Pocketed it. I pulled the door open with my fingertips.

Nothing. I pushed the bike bravely ahead, peeked out.

Nothing. I crept to the head of the stairs, shouldered the bike, creaked painstakingly down.

The hardest part was crossing the floor of the warehouse, then the yard. Every step was a fight to restrain myself from bolting, convinced that such blatant haste might precipitate something. So I walked as slowly as I could. Who was it said 'don't look behind, something may be gaining on you'? I knew just what he meant.

When I passed through the yard gates I jumped on the bike and pedalled off like the buggery. I nearly wobbled off, I was shaking so much.

I entered the address at ten to three.

The damn place was empty. It looked as though no one had been there for years. It was just the deserted basement of an old building, a repository for useless, worthless junk, pram wheels, beer cans, a gutted sofa. The place was a tomb, just waiting for the old building above to crumble into it.

I checked the address. It was the right place. I sighed. Now what?

I clambered back up the red stone steps, stood in the streaky sunshine on the street, letting the tired bike lean against me. I looked up and down.

I watched people walking about, reading newspapers, discoursing over bags of shopping, wheeling pushchairs, playing marbles along the gutters, floating matches in a shallow black puddle. None of them looked at me; I was one of them, an organ of the streetlife, as unremarkable as the sparrow that grubbed in a rain gutter.

Nobody thought to point me out, say, there's a man who doesn't know what to do, there's a man as lonely as a barrel on an ocean.

Someone was watching me, fifty yards away, hands in the high pockets of a too-small jacket so that his arms protruded like wings. I saw him twice before I recognized him. It was the reticent Harry. He jerked his head to have me follow.

He guided me to another house a quarter of a mile away, and in a first-floor room I was confronted by a cheerful Tommy and two other men, big, bruised, tenebrous men, like yetis in donkey jackets.

The three were seated at a table. A fourth chair waited to be occupied. I looked behind in time to see Harry pull the door closed on us.

'Sit down, cully,' said Tommy pleasantly. 'How yez getting on?'

I shrugged. 'Okay I guess.'

'You ready to make your first payment?'

'The first payment?' I mumbled.

'Sure, for isn't it two of yez wantin' to go? This is for you. Your fare.' He smiled crookedly.

I arched my eyebrows and shrugged again, for want of something better.

'Don't be so grum, cully,' said Tommy. 'It's not the end of the world.' He lit a cigarette, didn't offer me one. 'This is Michael by the way and Brennan.' They looked at me like two Saint Bernards and maybe nodded, the movement so slight it was hard to tell.

I said, 'Howdy.'

'Aye, we've found a job for you,' Tommy went on. 'A simple knockover.' A simple knockover? He made it sound like a game of skittles.

One of the other two, Brennan I think, suddenly offered me a photograph. 'Do you know him?' He had a voice like waves in a shingle cave.

I looked at the face and felt nothing. I shook my head. 'Should I?' Brennan shrugged.

Tommy said, 'He's the man. He'll be a pushover; cully, a pushover. Only take you five minutes.'

I stared at the picture in silence for a minute, trying

103

to figure out what the man had ever done to me that I should blow him away. I could think of no reason. I didn't think I could do it. 'What has he done? I can't just kill someone without knowing why.'

'He's too political,' said Tommy. 'A big wheel in the fascists. We don't like political policemen. Also, if it makes it any easier for you, he's a pervert. He's raped a couple of young girls, and boys. His name's Fitzwilliam.'

'Fitzwilliam!' I gasped. 'From Leyton Green?'

'You know the man?'

'No, I don't. I know of him though.' I stared at the picture, at the hard, hateful expression with the flat, saucer ears and the hare lip and the colourless eyes.

'Yeah,' I said grimly. 'I'll do it. I'll take out Fitzwilliam.' I only had to think of Rachel.

Tommy grinned. 'That's the way cully, hate the bastard, it'll make it easier.' He coughed in an unhealthy manner. 'Sure, it's as well you'll do it an' all, else we'd have to turn yez over to the authorities.' He offered me a smoke.

'How do I do it?'

'Sure, an' that's up to you and all, do whatever you like, we'll give you what you need. I'd suggest shooting him, but some folk like to blow 'em up, they say it's less personal. Meself I like the personal touch.'

'No,' I said. 'I'll shoot him.' Right between the piggy bastard eyes.

'Well look, now here's what we suggest. Tomorrow night he'll be at a brothel at 26 Mary Magdalene Street, between about seven and half-past eight. He goes there every Tuesday to beat up a little Jewish girl, but that's her lookout. Why don't you have a look at him, see what you think. See he might be off his guard then, relaxed like, he wouldn't be expecting anything.'

'Should he be expecting anything?' I asked suspiciously.

'Well, yes and no. See, someone tried to knock him
over a couple of weeks ago and he's got a couple of
bodyguards now – '

'Bodyguards!' I bawled.

'They're only lads off the street, they're no danger.
Go an' have a look at the place. If you don't like it we'll
maybe try something else.'

'There's a lot of empty rooms across the street,'
boomed Brennan. 'You could use a rifle. If you think
you could hit him.'

I thought about it.

'Will you give it a go, cully?'

I thought about it some more. There was nothing else
I could do. I nodded. 'Yeah, I'll go and have a look at
the guy. See if I can work something out. Do I – do I
have to go on my own?' I'm a guy who likes his hand
held.

'Aye, well our faces are known see, aren't they? This
is why we have to, as you might say, keep a low profile.
You go an' have a look, and one of us'll come round and
see yez in a couple of days, work it out.'

'Okay,' I murmured.

'Is there something wrong, cully?'

'Yeah. Who's Homer?'

'Homer? Never heard of him. Is it a riddle?'

'He's been asking after me. He's found out I'm at the
warehouse, he left this on my bed.' I showed them the
calling card. 'While I was sleeping in it.'

All three looked at the message, shook their heads in
turn.

'I can't go back there. I'm scared. You'll have to put
me someplace else.'

Tommy considered it. He sighed. 'It's not that easy, cully. These things need a lot of sorting out. It's probably just some nutter trying to scare you.'

'He's bloody succeeded.'

Tommy looked at the other two for a moment, then back to me. He took something from his pocket and put it down with a click in front of me. 'Take this cully,' he said sombrely. 'If he comes back, you can do a bit of scaring yerself.'

It was a revolver. Black, heavy and ominous. I stared at it with chilled fascination.

FIVE

Fitzwilliam came out of the brothel right on time, I think; I really must get a watch.

I watched him pause at the top of the nine steps beneath the grey-brown Victorian façade, behind the protective pair of goons. He looked a lot like his picture, even from where I stood in a doorway thirty yards away.

One goon – they were both dressed casually in slacks and windcheaters – skipped down the stones, opened the back of a black limo which waited with one wheel holding down the kerb. Fitzwilliam followed down, climbed in; the second goon eased in beside him.

The first goon hit the door, clicked round to the front, got in, gunned the engine. The car bumped away. The whole thing took just a few moments.

Of course recognizing Fitzwilliam is one thing; hitting the bastard and getting away unscathed is another. I blew out my cheeks as I pictured the scene again. How to distract the bulls, that was the problem.

I looked along the street but it didn't help much. Just a few desultory people walking places, the way people do. But when I glanced the other way, it came to me in a flash. I knew just what was needed.

By the way, Harry called round this afternoon in an old, battered blue van. He's teaching me to drive.

*

You're probably wondering how I feel at the prospect of killing Fitzwilliam. No? No matter, I'll tell you anyway.

I don't like it; but I figure I can live with it. He's a bastard.

At least this way I have some choice in who I kill. If I joined the army I'd have to kill who they told me to. Harmless little guys out of corner shops, pregnant women, kids with whooping cough or acne, little girls flushed with the thrill of their first boyfriend.

They don't care about it, do they? The desktop strategists, the militarist professors. At least I care. I feel responsibility. I feel shame. Those bastards don't go and kill anyone themselves, they do it all by proxy.

At least I'll kill someone deserving. Not a bloody innocent. Fitzwilliam's just a blemish on the human landscape. He's a bane. And a disease.

My life is hell at the moment. Every anxious hour torments me.

I'm exhausted, I looked at my pan in the mirror *ce matin* and I was watching the visage of an old man. This Homer has a lot to answer for.

It's not so bad when I'm out. But when I return to this place I feel like a hunk of meat in a lion's den.

I know he's coming back for me. Every minute I hear his footfall. I'm trapped in this room. I shake; I sweat; I slump down with vertigo.

I'm so scared I can only sleep in reluctant snatches and berate myself when I jerk awake. I've got myself into a right state.

I've barricaded the door with everything I can lay my paws on: lumps of concrete, bricks, bags of earth. I've taken the mattress from the bed and laid it against the farther wall in the corner opposite the door. And I've built a brattice of bricks to sleep behind, a yard high, a foot longer than the mattress. Sometimes I think I might as well be in the army, pinned in a foxhole.

I don't expect him to come through the window. I doubt he's a butterfly. But I reveal myself as seldom as possible. He might shoot me or he might be there just watching, which would be even worse. I'd rather be dead than dying.

My haunted mind has bestowed on Homer the

dimensions of a fabulous being, a minotaur, a god, a spectre. God, I haven't even seen the man, but I have a picture in my mind as clear as anyone I've ever known. Homer, the scarred albino, nearly seven feet tall, but quiet as a wraith, perhaps immortal. The Eternal Vengeance. The Haunter. The Hunter. (I later learned that Homer prefers to put his quarry to flight. If you try to escape Homer can kill you. And Homer likes to kill people.)

Conditions in my room are dreadful. I collected a pile of old paint tins which I use as toilets; when they're full I throw them out of the window. But I have to be careful with the water, I'm frightened to go out for any more.

I'm smoking about fifty a day now. Harry brings them for me. At least, he did yesterday. He said he'd be back again this afternoon with the van.

I wish he'd hurry. I'm a wreck. Really jittery.

SEVEN

This morning Homer came.

It was early. Perhaps about seven. A starling was croaking in the gutter above the window. The dawn was argent and cool, as if a day out of March had lingered on unsuspected.

I was lying on my back. Staring at the flaking ceiling. All its nicotine suntan was peeling off. I was thinking about America, wondering what it's really like.

All of a sudden I knew he was coming.

I don't know how I knew, perhaps I just intuited it. Perhaps my mind heard something my consciousness didn't register.

But hairs all over my body began to prickle. And my breathing stopped, like a rabbit on its haunches.

I was stiffer than a cobra. Every attribute of perception was a tense, screaming nerve, every nerve was taut as a crossbow, assuming command of the body so that my less spontaneous mind had to scamper to catch up. I felt my knotted guts unbind.

I lay there waiting, listening; surprisingly passionless. I remember thinking, 'So the bastard's coming at last.' Suddenly he didn't seem quite so divine. Perhaps that's a kind of desperation.

But for all that my hands were battened into rigid veined fists upon my belly and my teeth were clenched into a snarl. My straining concentration focused on a cynosural spot on the ceiling.

Ages, minutes passed, before I heard anything. It was the barest of creaks from the first rickety step. I knew it was the bottom step because its sound is much more hysterical than any of the others. There are sixteen of them. I waited for him to tick them off. But there was no more sound.

At the first movement I had rolled on to my right side, picked up the cold revolver that had been lying on the mattress beside me. It too never slept. It too lay and watched the ceiling. And waited.

I eased the hammer back but I didn't touch the trigger. My fingers were quivering too much.

Still no further noise penetrated the buffered door. But I felt the moment approach, draw close on patient footfall, as a slow storm that at dawn blackens the horizon and by midday is still not overhead.

I eased to my knees, stealthy as a ballerina. I shuffled my legs back on the mattress, squatted on my heels. Stiff-armed, I rested my hands and the metallic death on the double wall of bricks, and pointed the attentive cruel eye at the heart of the door. Held it quietly in check, like a hunting dog. I let my breathing slide in and out, as smoothly as a swell on the midsummer ebb tide.

The nervous door had its back to me. All its thought was on the intruder approaching. I saw it stiffen as it caught its breath.

The silence was like a great bell tolling, a tocsin deafening in the tiny grey room which shrank around me and kept me alive. I wondered where the enemy was. I feared he might appear through the wall behind me. Perhaps he would strangle me, without me ever

112

seeing his face, with fingers like steel hawsers grinding into my throat.

Twenty minutes must have passed since I detected the first deliberate creak. I couldn't figure out what he was doing; perhaps he was still on the first creaking step, frightened to move. I was growing stiff. I noticed the attentive gun had begun to sweat.

I had decided to change my position slightly when a gentle tapping killed the door stone dead, struck down by a violent heart attack. 'Who is it?' I demanded, as if all my life I'd been awaiting the chance to say it.

There was a long pause, fifteen seconds, twenty seconds. Half a minute. Then a wolf murmured a single, deathly word: 'Homer.'

To hell with what he might want, this guy was terrifying the wits out of me. I fired, blam blam blam blam! Four shots in quick succession, as fast as I could pump the eager trigger. So close together they sounded like one report.

The first two went where I intended, through the door, chest height above the knob; the third went up through the lintel, the fourth hit the wall by the light switch. It's not easy to control a revolver when you fire like that, the thing gets heavy, bucks around like an animal. If I'd fired all six I'd probably have wound up shooting myself.

There was silence then, though the air went on dumbly ringing. I stared horrified, as if expecting to see thick, crimson blood come welling out of the two raggedy holes in the door.

But nothing happened. No cry came, no retort, no reaction of any kind, except the wall of silence. It was as if I'd shot at a mirage.

The revolver began to shake in my grasp, gradually

infecting me, until my arms, then my whole body, were juddering violently. So violently that I knocked a couple of bricks out of the breastwork.

I lay down, letting the soft mattress absorb my shudders, waiting for something to happen. I had done my part, now it was up to Homer to make a move. Preferably by releasing his soul. I couldn't understand how he took it so quietly; even if I'd killed him he ought to have made some sound. A croak or something. I began to think that perhaps he really was a spectre.

I was terrified. There was no way I was going to clear that barricade or open the door. I remembered once hearing a tale about a group of people in medieval England who sealed themselves in a castle to escape the plague and wouldn't come out, even when their provisions had gone and they were starving. Because the plague put such a fear on them. Even when the pestilence was past, they wouldn't believe it. And slowly they starved to death.

Perhaps Homer is the plague, I thought. Perhaps he wants to frighten me to death.

I wiped the wet handle of the revolver, rearranged my grip on it. Two bullets left.

Three hours later maybe, I heard someone on the stairs. I must have been dozing. I panicked before I realized where I was.

I struggled to my knees, wedged my body into another firing position.

I listened as the squeaking, creaking ascended. There was no stealth now. If Homer was coming back he'd clearly decided to end the affair. On to the landing, three steps to the door, I knew them well. Then the tapping again.

'Are yez in there, Howard?' It was Tommy's voice. I saw the handle swoon as he rattled it. 'Howard? Jeez what are you doing boy, what's these bloody holes an' all?'

I grunted something incoherent, staggered up and dragged aside the barricade. I twisted the key, let a chary Tommy in.

'Sure what the bloody hell's been goin' on here?' he asked. 'By Christ, what's that smell? Can you not open the bloody window cully? What's been goin' on?'

I said, 'Did you see anybody out there? On the landing or the stairs?'

'Only me own two feet. Were you expecting someone?'

'Was there no blood?'

'Blood? None at all that I could see. Have you been shooting at people?'

'Homer. He came back this morning.'

'Homer? The guy who left the note? And what did he want?'

'I didn't ask him. He came to kill me.'

'Did he tell you that? Is that what he said now? Sure no wonder you popped off at him. Jeez, look at that hole in the wall, he must've been moving fast!'

I didn't say anything for a while, looking for justification. 'You've got to move me somewhere else, Tommy. I don't know who that guy is, but he's out to get me. I'm no use to anybody dead.'

'Aye, well maybe you're right. If you stay here much longer you're liable to shoot me or Harry. Get your things together, I'll take yez over to the lad's, he knows the places to stay. Did you get a good look at

Fitzwilliam the other day? Did you come up with anything?'

As I told Tommy my plan he picked up a scrap of paper from behind the door. When I'd finished packing he handed it to me.

It read, 'In your sleep Howard, in your sleep'.

EIGHT

This is Tuesday. At twenty past eight I am in Mary Magdalene Street.

There is a clear cobalt sky overhead. A fiery orange sun is descending. In the street many people are coming and going. Unaware that I bring violent death. That I am Shiva. The evening slayer.

I look up as a ragged V of gulls plods towards the estuary. I see a plane twinkle very high up. I see a big purple blob in the middle of the sun, and look away blinking.

I fidget in my pockets.

I'm in the doorway of an empty house twenty yards below the brothel at number twenty-seven, on the opposite side of the street.

Sixty yards above number twenty-seven, on my side of the street, stands a second-hand clothes store, beside an alleyway. It's empty, the owner went home an hour ago. Up above is a flat. Which is also empty. Next door is a fish-and-chip shop, habited by a varying number of people, at the moment seven. The store is called 'Odds and Sods'. It is in its last few minutes.

In the darksome doorway of 'Odds and Sods' crouches a plain plastic carrier. It loiters like someone waiting for a date. I pray that no one's tempted to have a gander, for inside is a small bomb and a can of paraffin. An electronic detonator in the device is

117

operated from a little gizmo in my pocket. In my other pocket is my revolver, (note that I now say *my* revolver; humans are quick to become possessive) now fitted with a stubby grey silencer.

I twiddle with the silencer while I wait. In my other pocket the gizmo grows slippery with sweat. I tell a curious kid to buzz off; when he won't go I frighten him away with a torrent of bad language. I'm in no mood for gawking eyes.

At eight twenty-five my heart does a flip as the brothel door swings inward. But it's just one of the girls going for chips. A dog cocks its leg over a wheel of the dusty black limo. I curse time for being so laggardly.

There is another movement in the entrance and I prepare myself again. My heart races, bubbles of gelid sweat prickle all over the skin. I glance up the road. Oh Jesus, an old woman has stopped right by the primed doorway, she's stooped, doing something to one of her shoes.

My eyes race back to the brothel. The first of Fitzwilliam's heavies has appeared, he's talking to someone over his shoulder. I pour vitriol on the old, pathetic woman. Move you stupid cow. Move you bugger.

Goon the Second steps out, laughing. Fitzwilliam's right behind, lighting a black cigarette from a cupped palm.

The old woman starts retying her other bleeding shoelace. Jesus Christ, I can't believe this is happening. They come down the steps, they're not hurrying, they're all in a good mood, I can hear them joking. Fitzwilliam's laugh rises above the banter.

The old woman has put her bag down so that she can

118

devote more attention to her shoe. I'm grinding my teeth to powder.

The little kid reappears, starts throwing used matches at me. How cute. The goon opens the door, leans for a moment on the car, listening to Fitzwilliam's joke. My nerves scream at the painstaking crone who's checking in her handbag now.

Finally she moves. She turns into the alley, shuffles on her way. I speed back to the limo. Fitzwilliam is just twisting into the back, another couple of seconds would be too late. I hit the button.

Woomph! The doorway erupts with a mighty bang and a rush of fire. For a moment it stuns me, much louder, much closer than I anticipated. The whole street seemed to jump in an abnegation of guilt, from the rooftops down to the roadway. There came an almost instantaneous echo from the houses opposite, before all their windows blew in.

I'm not looking at the clothes store, my attention is on the group at the limo. But from the corner of my eye I see a pale, gaseous flame gout thirty feet across the street to spill a purple ochre flame along the pavement. Even the concussion wave seems to rebound. And as I spring down the three steps to street level I have to look at the damage I've wrought.

The frontage of 'Odds and Sods' a moment after the explosion is ablaze. Fire scampers in at the ripped-out windows and out again. Serpents of flaming paraffin writhe on the street and pavement and fill the air with haze.

People are fleeing, darting in all directions; the fish-and-chip shop spews screamers into the evening, retches itself empty. Faces look from the glassless windows of the houses opposite, like little pigs wondering why the wolf should pick on them.

A child's pram parked outside the chip shop is ignited. Fortunately it's empty. The kid with the box of used matches goes pelting up the street to have a closer look. Let's hope he falls into the flames. I start to cross the pandemoniac street.

The door slams behind Fitzwilliam and he twists on the seat to stare out wanly at the uproar. Before he's even figured out what's happening the first goon is sprinting along the street, bent almost double, gun drawn. He moves with amazing speed and before I've even reached the car he has vaulted a wall and is splayed behind it, eager gun ranging over the scene, hungry for a target.

The other bodyguard is crouched behind the car, all I can see of him is the back of his head, but I can hear him shouting to his buddy. He sounds a bit panicky, I wouldn't trust him in an emergency.

I stride up to the car with horrifying complacency; once I'd started the event seemed to have taken me over. It's all I can do to hold from whipping out the gun prematurely. I clear my throat, a nervous habit.

I walk right up to the offside door and stoop to look inside. Fitzwilliam doesn't see me, he's still engrossed in my arson, doesn't know whether it's to do with him or not. I take a picture out of my pocket, hold it to the window. It's a photograph of Gay.

I tap with my knuckles. Fitzwilliam's face snaps around full of alarm. I point at the picture, mouth a few words. The alarm relaxes fractionally to wariness and he looks puzzled. What? his expression says.

I mouth again, pointing at the picture as if it's important. He shuffles forward, pushes a button to slide the window down, starts to say, 'What the f . . .'

I rip the gun out. Before he can say uh-oh it's sticking in his face, right at the top of his nose, digging into the flat hairy skin between his eyes raising wrinkles all around.

I watch the colour drain from his lips as though someone has pulled a plug. I'm staggered by the disbelief in his gaze; people really can't believe it's happening.

He tries to lick his lips, but his tongue's as dry as eggshell, it just laps at the air like a nervous gecko. I jab the gun more fiercely, to give me courage.

I try to focus all of my hatred on to the weapon and the moment. And I succeed, but it's not enough. I can't pull the trigger. I let the pressure on his face ease slightly, but he cannot notice it, all he sees is death.

I hiss at him. 'Who is Homer?'

'Homer?' he gasps weakly, after a moment. 'Homer?'

I stab again with the gun, and this time I bring a tear to his right eye. 'Who is he?'

'Homer.' I can see him running over lists of names in his mind. His lips tremble. 'Homer,' he mumbles after an eternity. 'The albino. He's with the army. He's a hunter. A hunter.' His voice sounds like the wind under a door. 'Real name's Rickardson.'

I want to pull the trigger. God I really want to pull it. But I've waited too long, I can feel all the fragile resolve splintering apart.

The silencer begins to vibrate, slowly at first, as if it's looking for a precise spot. But then more wildly, up and down, until it's waving all over the top of his face and my whole arm is trembling. I begin to dither, my teeth start to chatter.

Fitzwilliam doesn't look at me, his eyes are locked by the demented black cynosure, by the tiny bottomless hole that will ignite and fill with death; by the havoc of his brain which quivers inches from his skull. No wonder he can't look away.

I can't stand the tension, I think I'm going to scream.

I snatch the gun away, lower it to my side. For the first time Fitzwilliam looks at me, with eyes expressionless, but fearful of his fate. I abhor him, my whole body chokes on the emotion, the forepart of my brain explodes with pounding thunder. But the storm will not erupt.

Suddenly he darts forward, stabs at the window button. I watch it begin to slide up, whining. Now Fitzwilliam's face is racked with dread, he thinks his hope may be false. . . .

At last I respond, wheel on the spot and pound away. I hear Fitzwilliam's voice behind, shouting, then a gun fires and a bullet whizzes past my shoulder on its hasty way to an appointment.

But at the same instant I'm turning a corner into another street. I sprint down there a short way, turn into a narrow alley. I cross another street, echo along another alley, and a blue van is waiting for me. I dive in.

The van roars, races momentarily on the spot and zooms away. Suddenly I vomit.

'Did you do it?' asked Harry as he steered the van into a breakneck turn.

I clung to the door for support. 'No,' I said thickly. 'I couldn't make it.'

'I don't blame you,' said Harry, fighting to keep us on an even keel as another screeching turn hove towards us. 'I've never killed anyone myself. I wouldn't like to shoot someone in the head.'

'How would you do it?'

He steered us off a pavement and eased up a little on the throttle. 'I'd poison a rat, and train the bugger to bite him.'

I laughed, thought about it, laughed some more. It was a relief to uncork the pressure.

'I found out who Homer is.'

'Aye?'

'He's with the army. A hunter Fitzwilliam called him.'

'I've heard about them,' said Harry. 'They're hard bastards. They only recruit psychopaths.'

'Thanks a lot.' We laughed some more.

'Now you'll have Fitzwilliam after you as well.'

'He won't know me.'

'Did you show him the picture of your girl? How many people do you think have a picture like that?'

It was a sombre thought. As if I didn't have enough to worry about, with the vomit all over my boots and all.

'You'll have to finish him next time.'

'Next time?' I hadn't thought that far yet.

'Sure, they gave you a job to do. It's still to be done. That's how they look at it.'

I watched dowdy terraces roll by, looked at the black-bag heaps of rubbish waiting for a collection which seldom comes. I noticed a couple of rats playing about on one pile.

London looked as dismal as I felt. What had happened to the nice evening? When I looked up I couldn't see the sun, it had slipped behind a ribbon of cloud on the horizon.

'Do you ever think we're in the wrong game?' I asked.

Harry thought a moment before replying. 'I don't

think we're even in the right room.' He let the van slow right down while we had a look at some commotion at a crossroads. It looked like a street fight. 'We wanted the billiards room and we ended up in the bog.' We picked up speed as someone lobbed a lump of concrete at us. It bounced off the roof.

'I wanted to kill him. I really wanted to. Right up to the moment the trigger pressed into my finger, I could have done it. But then I couldn't. If he'd only screamed or cried or begged or something, I would have done it. But I couldn't kill him in all that silence. All that commotion was going on around, and it was quiet as the grave.'

Harry, who can be fairly laconic at times, nodded thoughtfully. 'I'm like that with a chick. If it's too quiet, I just can't make it.' He braked outside a tenny block and cut the engine. 'I think I get embarrassed. I'm better if there are people around.'

We went indoors.

I've been staying with Harry since I left the warehouse.

NINE

Eight days later. Harry and me have been shadowing Fitzwilliam for four days.

He has become my only close friend, Harry. He doesn't have to help me, he's not an activist, he works with cars, fixes people up. But he's put himself in the firing line with me. With his shy brown eyes and his slight frame, he's the best friend I've ever had.

It's not easy tailing someone by van. Sometimes we're the only other vehicle you see on the road all day. But Harry eases us around like a cat, hugging walls, dashing across intersections.

We've discovered that every other day, on his way home from work, Fitzwilliam buys a load of booze from a little store.

Today is an other day. Harry and me, we're waiting for him. Just around a corner from the little shop. There's about half an hour to go. We're sitting quietly, smoking.

Harry came from Newry. He was born there twenty years ago, his mother was a schoolteacher, his father an IRA recruiter. At fifteen he came to England with a cousin who was killed in the Edmonton riots. He's surprisingly shy, very softly spoken.

'Why don't you come to America with us Harry?'

Harry thought about it for a while, in the pensive way he thinks about everything. 'Nar,' he murmured at

125

last. 'I don't think so, Bart. I think America's too big for me, I'd get lost.

'Besides they wouldn't let me. After a while they think you belong to them. They're very possessive.'

'You don't like it though do you?' He's very relaxing, Harry. I felt as though we'd been sitting there for ever, just talking.

He crunched a mint. 'Sure. Who likes what they do?' Suddenly he swung his feet down from the dash and sat up. 'Here he is. It's Fitzwilliam. He's early today.'

I spat out my mint, I could do without all that crunching in my head. I stubbed out a smouldering butt.

'Get the grenade.'

I fingered the warm cylinder as I closed the door behind me, walked the twenty feet to the corner, peered warily around.

There was the limo, parked about fifteen yards up the way. Bugger, I'd hoped it would be closer than that. Fitzwilliam's bull was just entering the store. There wasn't much time to think about it. Probably just as well. I set off. I could hear Harry turning the little van around behind me.

I twiddled a little device in my nervy left hand.

I closed rapidly on the back of the limo. Fitzwilliam and his driver stared ahead, oblivious to my approach.

The cylinder grenade in my right pocket had come from Brennan. It was about an inch in diameter, four inches long, with a metal button on the top. When I pushed the button I had eight seconds to get the hell out of there. Theoretically. Harry said the things are famed for unreliability. Thanks a lot Harry.

These big cars are too heavy to blow from the

outside. You have to get your explosion inside. That's one of the reasons I was sweating like an eel. I flipped open the flap of the petrol cap and jabbed a lock-break in; it's a flat key welded to a metal grip. You just ram it into the keyhole and twist until the lock breaks; kids use them to steal petrol.

I can tell you, I twisted that grip like my life depended on it. There was a clunk as the togs sheared off. I spun the cap, wrenched it off. It took less than a second to push the button and drop the grenade into the fuel tank.

I turned, walked away.

I could picture the scene behind me. Fitzwilliam would have heard the noise, he would have heard the grenade tumble into the tank. He'd be wondering what the sound was. Probably looking after me, wondering who I was, maybe even recognizing me. He had about seven seconds to save his life. Maybe he'd have a word with the driver. He'd probably realize suddenly that something was wrong. Take a second to figure that out, a second of fear.

Four seconds, I counted.

Then I suddenly realized that the way I was walking I'd be only about a dozen yards away when the bloody thing blew. I ran.

Five seconds. Six. I was almost at the corner. I heard someone shout behind me, maybe it was Fitzwilliam, maybe it was the bull, I don't know.

I flung myself around the corner. Voom!!! It sounded like a bomb had fallen right at my heels. A boot lid bounced off the road a few feet away.

I sprinted across the road, dived into the creeping van. We shot down the road. About a hundred yards away we screeched to a halt and looked back.

Nothing. We couldn't see anyone following us.

We waited a minute, then Harry spun the van around and sped back to the corner. He braked right on the intersection and we looked up the road.

Wow. It was a great place to collect vehicle souvenirs. The limo was splattered all over the place. Corrida. The bull was dead.

I saw the store window had been ripped out – strange that, I thought it would have blown in. There was glass everywhere. And lumps of burned metal, all the paintwork must have been instantly conflagrated.

A leg was lying not far away, twitching. Maybe it was a trick of the flames, they were skittering all over the road, clinging on to lumps of the broken car like fungus. A writhe of capricious smoke drifted back and forth; it reminded me of an old matron. And everywhere there were bits of car or body to be looked at. There must have been a thousand, ten thousand pieces scattered about. Some were even stuck to the walls of the buildings. One sheet of metal had landed on somebody's roof, and plenty of folk must have had pieces of bodywork or bodyguard lying in their front-rooms.

If Fitzwilliam survived that, he was God.

They began to appear then, the doorway echoes, the window spectres. The tragedy vampires. The catastrophe vultures. Some of them looked at us rather charily, as if they expected us to explode next.

We roared off.

TEN

Yesterday we had a day out. Harry had to deliver a couple of boxes of stuff to some bazonka in Earls Court. We took Rachel along and made a day of it.

I like travelling through central London, it's like going back to a home I only vaguely remember, very familiar, yet very strange. *Presque vu.*

It is still an exciting place, though much of it has run down now. Like clockwork models whose keys have been lost. You have to picture what it was like when they were all in motion. You have to try to people the abandoned offices and timeless stores with a new race of ghosts, people without substance replacing the people without pneuma.

We made a game of counting the restaurants and cafeterias still open between Leytonstone and Westminster. There were eleven. That's the sort of place it's become. The number boarded up approached triple figures.

Tourists don't come any more. That kind of London – the gifts, the crap, the money for old soap, the razzmatazz – that's all gone. All the gay bright lights have melted down. All the gay young blades have dulled to become alcoholics or hustlers, or gone to war to find solace and refuge in a muddy French grave or a Hungarian dyke.

That's the way of things; all things crumble for him

who waits. I remember my mother telling me about the day Tower Bridge collapsed. It's still there today, blocking half the river. At low tide you can practically walk across.

Conversely, there is still a lot going on. There is still a country to be run, a city to be fed and entertained. But nobody does it with any joy, it's a sullen, resentful, recreant affair. Every smile is a cold-eyed mask, every offer is a challenge to accept.

Take Christmas. Nobody puts any coloured lights up. There are no fir trees filling the store windows or shedding needles on people on windy street corners. No cheery plastic Santas bobble about on lampposts and wires. No invisible choirs Noël you through the streets. It could be 15 January, or 11 February. It's an event of non-eventful proportions.

This is what we live in. The Age of Demoralization.

We watch for a glimmer of sunrise on the murky horizon. Or a red tongue of sunset. The awakening eye, the ravening mouth. It's all the same. Live or die we can but try to make it through each day. Or avenge our race's dead.

But enough of this acrimony, let's get back to London. It's flatter than it used to be; a good many office blocks and what-have-you have been torn down to make way for plots of vacant, derelict ground. And it is also more secretive since lots of windows have been boarded up with mysterious, cold bits of plywood and cardboard, so that nobody knows what goes on within.

We dropped the boxes off at the pad, spent a little time wandering around the museums, which is boring as hell but we thought it traditional, and wound our way up to the park.

Had a good day there. Watched the gulls process

across the sky in wavy childish lines. Watched the ragged ducks blow their noses in the lake.

The sky bled brightness, quivered in its torment; so hot you could burn your fingers. The sun was explosive, like the coming of Christ, it strung the thin clouds out until they were just ripples on a blue beach. We took our shirts off to escape the rage.

Had a good day. But, I don't know, there always seems something so desperate about enjoying yourself. You enter into it with a kind of frenzy, a frenetic urgency as though you're not entirely convinced or sincere. It's not easy to be at liberty. Prisoners have it easy.

So hot though. All the grey faces shone with a greasy pallor. Everyone lay down on the grass as though it was their duty.

The riot trucks patrolled warily, nervous of this sweltering gathering. The soldiers in their uniforms sweated like pigs. They looked like pigs with their squinting eyes and their hot ears magnified by their short, spiky hair. One of them had a bikini top tied to the end of his rifle.

A fat man fell over gasping and couldn't breathe. I think maybe it was a heart attack. Nobody knew what to do so they all formed a concerned circle for him to die in. He was twitching round like a fish out of water, gargling in his nose. A couple of medics ran up from an aid hut, but he was a corpse by then, flat and peaceful, looking healthier than when he was alive. He was so fat they couldn't lift the stretcher, and they dragged it as if it was a litter. He left a stain on the flattened grass.

But that aside it was a good day. Someone was releasing balloons and they soared into the sky like the hopes of all the upturned faces, drifting off towards Kensington with a disturbing impassivity. That's the trouble with balloons, they have no expression. I'd much prefer to see the damn things burst, they look so flaming cocky.

We wanted to take a boat out on the lake but a crowd of rowdy skins took them all over and made everyone uneasy. That's the trouble, there's always someone ready to spoil it for you. I hoped the bastards would hurt themselves, but that sort never seems to. Goddamn yobbos. I can't see the meek inheriting the earth. There are too many hard buggers waiting to take it off them.

Harry and Rachel got on well. I think his broguish charms have won her over. The sly old fox.

Today was a day for sorting out loose ends and opening up some new ones.

Concerning the former I have perhaps a modicum of control over the little destinies involved. Perhaps. But with the latter I'm an impotent participant, dragged blindly along like flotsam in a maelstrom. Just a kitten for kismet. I cannot see what's coming; with hindsight, I learn little or nothing to benefit me in the future.

It is a grim turn when you cannot learn from hindsight. You feel futile, bootless; the weight of the universe burdens you like a rampant devouring disease for which you possess no contradiction. You feel as though you are failing not only yourself, but all of mankind. Your soul slips from you into the power of another.

At least, that's how I feel. Maybe I'm just a prick, I don't know.

I haven't seen Aunt Melanie since the second night I

spent over there, when she tried to persuade me into Franklyn's side of the sheets.

It was a bad scene that, I'd felt disappointed about it. Disappointed for her, disappointed with her, disenchanted with myself. We'd both let ourselves down. It was kind of embarrassing. And bloody sad. I didn't feel good about not going back. I should at least have told her.

I've felt pretty bad about it ever since. I thought she was being cunning; I thought she was underestimating me. But it was just loneliness. She didn't want to be on her own.

And I was the great intellectual, too proud, too wise to stoop to her humble fears. Too busy bloody moralizing about my own pathetic, unimaginative actions to listen. I'd fallen into that fatal, predictable trap of overestimating myself.

Like I said, I felt rotten about it. Sometimes I really hate myself. Though even that's indulgence. Goddammit, I even hate myself for hating myself.

I took her a couple of Mars Bars when I went over, as a little present. There would have been three, but I ate one on the way. Satan would have had no trouble getting me to eat his loaves of bread.

It was mid-afternoon. Harry had taken Tommy and Moose to a meeting in Hackney. I was meeting him later on outside the old Leyton Odeon; he wanted me to go with him to the Alhambra, just in case Rachel was there. He'll probably want me to sit and hold his jacket if he ever gets around to getting into bed with her. I just hoped she wasn't sitting there with some client.

I feel like an agent. Or a panderer. Joe Gooseberry.

By the way, I wanted to tell you how I feel about the death of Fitzwilliam.

I try not to think about it.

If I do I try to consider it as an event, rather than concerning people, fellow men, fellow flesh and blood, and guts, and ruptured eyeballs, and soaking wallets, and bits of shoelace and foot strewn all over a gawping, silent, mincemeat street.

Because I am not a killer. That is to say, I do not have the mentality of a killer. The murder nature.

Perhaps that's just a plea for absolution, I don't know. Maybe I'm just deluding myself. I don't have nightmares about it. I don't wake screaming and wet. But, nor can I view it unemotionally.

So I try not to think of it at all. And if I do, I concentrate on the immortal, if you like insentient parts of the experience; the pad of my boots, the warmth of the grenade in my palm, the lock-break which I dropped as I hurried away, the voom! of the explosion and the rush of hot air, the boot lid sliding like a tennis racquet on the tarmac behind me. I only think of Fitzwilliam and his driver and the guy coming out of the store if I'm feeling brutal.

Then I can shift the blame on to them, let a bitter anger overwhelm the culpability. But if I'm to be truly honest, in a year from now I'll feel no remorse at all. It will be as if I was a different person, no longer to be held responsible. For thus do we excuse the crimes of our existence, the weekly, daily, hourly sins, the inhumanity of our mortal souls. Below, I am a murderer. Above, I would never lower myself to such a thing. You explain it.

All I can tell you is, I was more worried about facing Aunt Mel than confronting my conscience. My conscience I can lie to, but Aunt Mel can see my face.

She looked kind of awkward when she let me in.

Awkward, embarrassed and kind of dishevelled, as if someone had been practising knots with her hair. She also had bruises on her throat. And a new necklace.

My suspicions were confirmed when I entered the living-room. There was a newspaper on the coffee table. Aunty Mel can't read.

'Sit down Barty,' she said, smiling. 'Would you like a cup of tea?'

'Yes. Sure.' I stood up as a man came into the fusty room, a short wiry bloke, about Mel's age, a little older maybe, with a lot of stubble and dandruff on his greasy black hair. The sort of bloke you find in betting shops and men's toilets.

He grunted something incomprehensible, tucking a pinstripe shirt into the top of a pair of baggy grey trousers and I replied in similar fashion. Poor Aunt Mel's embarrassment was burning like a fire. 'This is Gerald, Barty,' she said. 'Gerald, this is Barty.'

Gerald sat down without glancing at me, picked up the newspaper and started looking through the pictures in the fashion of a true appraiser, squinting through a wraith of smoke. It took me a minute to figure out where the wraith was coming from; then I realized Gerald had a smouldering butt tucked behind his ear.

I couldn't help wondering whether he left it there when he made love with pneumatic Aunt Mel.

Probably he just carried on smoking.

I don't think I liked him.

Mel clattered about in the kitchen and after a minute I went out to join her. I patted her in a fairly matey fashion on the bum. 'How are you doing then, Mel? You okay?'

She smiled, nodded gamely. 'Sure Barty. Sure I am. You?'

'Oh, okay I guess. Okay. You know.'

'I got tired of waiting for you,' she said, shovelling tea from a caddy to a pot. 'I figured you wouldn't be back.'

'Only passing through. I wasn't planning on staying.' I filched a biscuit from the jar. 'That Gerald, is he your type?' God, I wish I didn't say things like that. I really wish I didn't.

Mel took a few moments to reply. 'What's anybody's type? He keeps the bed warm. He eats my meals.'

I shrugged. 'A dog'd eat your meals.' She slapped me hard, right across the front of my face. It came right out of the blue, I hadn't anticipated it at all.

'I'm sorry Mel,' I mumbled. 'I didn't mean to start in on you. It just took me off balance, him being here and all.' I really was sorry, I don't know what I thought I was doing. Maybe it was my pride, maybe I was just jealous. Jealous, of a poor little weedy guy like Gerald.

'I'm sorry too,' mumbled Mel. 'I didn't mean to hurt you.' She started cutting up a loaf, for no real reason other than something to do.

'I came to say I'll likely be going away soon.'

'They haven't caught you then?'

'Not yet. Maybe they won't now.'

'Do you need some money?'

'No, thanks. I can manage.'

'Where will you go?'

'America probably. Anywhere away from the war.'

She switched the kettle off, poured the scalding bellyfull into the pot. 'I enjoyed it you know, what we did.'

'So did I,' I said, mostly truthfully. I can't pretend I didn't at the time.

'All those years,' she said. 'All those years I dreamed

136

and wondered. And then we did it twice, and you're gone.'

What could I say? I kept quiet.

She bit some hard skin from around a nail. 'Like waiting for Christmas.' She put a cosy on the pot. 'Christmas ain't so bloody good when it comes, is it?'

I was on the brink of getting out of my depth here, so I remained quiet. I didn't want to appear stupid, but I wasn't sure I was keeping up with this conversation.

'What if I was pregnant?'

'What?'

'I won't be of course. But what if I was?'

'I, er, don't know.'

'What would you do if I had a little boy and called it Barty?'

'I, er, I guess I'd send it a birthday present.'

She half laughed. 'I had a baby once.'

'A baby? I didn't know.'

'A little girl. She died after three weeks.'

I lit a cigarette, remembered myself just in time and offered one to Mel. She nodded for me to light it for her.

'Do you want to know how she died?'

I wasn't sure I did.

'I passed out as I was putting her in her cot. I fainted a lot the first few weeks after the birth. I suffocated the poor bastard.' She was quite calm about all this, she wasn't getting upset or anything. I couldn't understand why she was telling me.

'When was this?'

'Oh ages ago. When you were a little lad in short trousers and a sulky lip.' She started pouring the tea. 'She had the same birthday as you. That's funny isn't it?'

'I guess so.'

'I always thought that, one day, I'd have your child. You know, to sort of make up for it. Like our fates were intertwined. You know what I mean?'

I shook my head helplessly.

'But it was a fool idea, wasn't it? We weren't intertwined at all. It was just a bloody coincidence.' She handed me my cup. 'Fate, it's a load of shit. It's a load of bloody shit.'

Here's a crazy thing. We didn't kiss each other at all when we said good-bye. We shook hands. Do you think that's weird? We shook hands in the doorway. We were strangers.

I didn't even promise to write or anything.

There would be no point anyway, she can't read. Still, it seemed a very abrupt way of ending a lifelong relationship. Maybe I'll just send her a Christmas card every year. Then again, maybe I won't. I'll have to think about all this some other time.

When I left I still had the Mars Bars in my pocket. Funny how things never turn out the way you expect. I asked someone the time. A while to go before I met Harry. I started to walk. Nowhere in particular, just killing the old minutes, wandering around like an old pigeon.

I came on to the brow of a hill, surrounded by waste land. A landscape of rubble and just me and a solitary burned-out house stood above it. Like the last pavilion on a battlefield.

I stood there with my hands in my pockets and looked, and felt, bloody miserable. I wondered where everybody had gone. Millions of people all around, and

I couldn't see anyone. Just this desolate echo, a circle of abandonment half a mile in diameter.

Buildings look like nothing at all when they're demolished. They die in amorphous shapes. They could have been anything, breweries, monasteries, post offices, undertaker's. You couldn't name them. But this rubble looked like the dead of houses, drab, monotonous, huddling.

Beyond, the city continued undisturbed. I was at a crossroads, four strips of pitted tarmac descended into the wilderness, picked their way into the rigid madness in which we hide.

I ate one of the Mars Bars.

What a gloomy day. If I was a bird, I'd be a million miles away.

A tribe of kids spilled out of a hole in a wall a couple of hundred yards below, shrieking like banshees. They started to beat hell out of a can with rocks and sticks.

A woman appeared pushing a pram. She began to plod up the hill towards me. She had a headscarf on. I saw that her blouse was coming out of the top of her skirt.

I turned another way. A building was smoking, over towards West Ham. Someone was hanging out washing above a flat roof, pink sheets were kicking feebly in the slight breeze. A skylight twinkled.

This is my home. This is the world I inhabit. Falling apart. I turned again, a full half circle. Homer waited, twenty yards from me.

I nearly gagged on the Mars Bar.

A screaming started up in my ears. Only in my mind, but it was deafening. I felt my skin go clammy. I couldn't swallow.

I began to back away.

Homer just watched. The tall albino made no move. Except to turn his head aside long enough to spit out a piece of pink gum.

I backed away another couple of paces.

The man had on a pair of loose, faded jeans, a short leather jacket over a white T-shirt. His running shoes looked new, they were bright blue.

He had shaved his head. A mountainous, bald, unblinking albino, intent on murder. Just what I needed. This was the first time I'd seen him. He was worse than I'd imagined. Much worse.

His hands were resting casually on his hips. His mouth was pursed, appraising; like a guy with a greyhound sizing up another man's dog. I don't think he had much to fear. As dogs go, I make a good rabbit.

But I couldn't stand this weird vigil. I whirled and bolted. More like a dachshund than a bloody racer.

I hurtled down that hill like a streak of spit, long legs pumping like a runaway train. Past the woman with the startled pram, a glimpse of her frightened eyes rolling after me, past a flash of unhealthily yellow skin, the rattle of a kid's toy.

I pounded down the crazy cracks and reached the first wall of the waiting world. Here at least I stood a chance; in the vastness of the desolation I was helpless. I risked a look over my shoulder. And stopped.

Homer was pursuing. But he was just walking down the hill. Steadily. But without any sign of haste. He was just walking. Already I was a couple of hundred yards ahead. I was at the end of the straight and he was still in the trap.

Why didn't he run? Didn't he want to end it? It was creepy. I began to slink away, my back pressed to the face of the first terraced house. And still Homer descended at the same leisurely pace. Nothing seemed to perturb him. He didn't need running shoes, he needed a sedan.

I couldn't stand it. I ran again.

At the farther end of the street – how far was that, a quarter of a mile? – I looked back. There he was, just entering. Walking. His eyes fixed on me. I could see them, pits of purple fire, blazing.

I turned a corner, bolted once more. Must keep on familiar ground I told myself. If I get lost, I'm done for. Must keep to where I know, don't let him steer me on to his territory.

But what if this was his territory? No time to worry about that, stick to what you know.

Already I had a stitch in my left side, didn't know whether to try to outrun it or wait until it cleared. Bloody agony. Carried on running. Looked back. There he was again. He must be walking faster now. Took another turn.

I'd been running for half an hour and I wasn't gaining anywhere. It was uncanny. Homer hadn't stretched to anything in excess of a steady jog, and yet he was right behind. He was clinging to me like a *Doppelgänger*, like something linked to me with chains.

My goddamn lungs were going up in flames, my nightmare throat was raw. I wheezed like an old tree in a gale. This wasn't fun at all. I was getting desperate.

Also, my ankles were feeling decidedly weak. Much more of that concrete pounding would cripple them. I needed to crawl into hiding. But couldn't get far enough ahead to find a place. I looked back. There he was again, a hundred yards adrift and steady as a rock, the bastard.

Which way to go? If I wasn't careful I'd lose all control of my ideas, I had to keep the panic at a low level. Keep it at a low level, that's a joke, I was on the verge of screaming.

Finding it so difficult to see clearly I thought my eyes must be bleeding. I had to do something, this was just crazy. The man was insane.

When an open builder's lorry rumbled past I flung myself at it without thinking. I caught hold of the side and dangled helplessly, feeble legs trailing along the street like two bits of rope. It was agonizing, but it was taking me away from Homer. I bit my lip until the tears poured down and dug my fingers into the sharp, rusty metal, to the bone.

I chanced a look back. Homer was in the road, sprinting now. Christ, he ran like a flaming gazelle! For one dreadful moment I thought he could catch the lorry, but we swung around a bend and when he appeared again he was further back. Still running though.

I tried to forget about him, tried to concentrate on clinging on through the jagged bumps and judders. Tried to keep my feet up. I was in agony. I was being crucified. God, what a nightmare. I wailed.

I hung on for a mile, then my precarious grip jettisoned me, still wailing. No wonder people were looking at me.

I would probably have let go anyway, my crutch was being bashed against the fuel tank and a red smog was starting to confuse my senses.

'Oof!' I rolled in the gutter, cracked my head on the kerb. If I had any wind left it was knocked out then. I think I also lost a tooth, but that may have happened later; whatever, my mouth was full of blood. So was my nose. My knuckles weren't, they were losing it fast.

I lay there groaning, hoping that this was all eidetic and I was really dead. But I dragged me back to myself and sat up. Homer. How fast could he run? More immediately, how far would he run?

What was all this in front of me? It was just my tortured vision, struggling to find a level on the seasick street.

At last the area loomed back into view, and a lot of gawking people too. Thank God Homer wasn't one of them, but I had such a respect for the man I expected him to appear at any instant. Physically he seemed inhuman. I suppose that's training. The only training I'd had was in being scared. And right at that moment I was graduating with distinction. Holy Mary, mother of God. Pray for us sinners. Now, and in the day of our death.

I hoped this wasn't it.

I stumbled to unsteady feet, looked around for guidance. As usual there was none.

I stuffed a few breaths into my pumping chest. God, pain everywhere. In every nook and cranny a little nag or twinge lurked. Some were big nags, big twinges. I felt like a laboratory. With some pretty cruel experiments going on.

I figured the route of the lorry had been reasonably straight, so set off at a tangent, hobbling as fast as I could. Stopped for a pee in a smelly alleyway.

Suddenly I recognized where I was. I put on a spurt; not easy when you're going flat out but I dragged it from somewhere. Sweat flowed like spring thaw.

I turned left, right, toddled a straight half mile;

across a bridge, across the corner of a playing field, under a bridge; down a hill, nearly ran under an ambulance, took a short cut over a wall, was chased out of someone's garden.

I emerged in a fairly busy thoroughfare, hustled through the stupid crowd. Get out of the way you bastards, leper coming. Saw something waiting a quarter of a mile ahead. A blue van. Harry's van.

I ran towards it. Snorting like a mating pig. Oh thank God for Harry's mother, and grandmother, and grandfather, and every spawn and relation back into the gob of time. Thank God for Ireland and the cows and the Guinness.

Harry saw me coming and jumped out. He came running to meet me, looked as worried as a priest. 'Jesus, Beekay, what in hell's name happened to ye? Mother of God you look like a nightmare.'

I grabbed his arm. 'Homer,' I croaked. 'We have to get out of here.'

He threw me into the van, pissed down the road like we were on fire.

If I hadn't been lying on the floor I'd have gone straight out the door the way we took that first bend.

And he wasn't even after Harry.

Back at the pad we threw everything we had on to the bed. We don't have suitcases, naturally, so everything was bundled up in bedsheets and we staggered down and out to the van looking like we were on our way to the laundry.

We needed four sheetsful; dumped the first two in the back, raced up the stairs for the remainder.

I was just on the point of following Harry down the

144

second time, when something stepped out of the hallway shadows right into my buddy's path. Homer! something screamed.

Harry tried to shout a warning. 'Beekay! Look – ' He choked off as a huge, thunderclap fist smashed into the cloud of his belly and lifted him off the ground. As he ricked up an unnecessary backhand burst his cheek and spun him around. Just watching, my whole body lurched. It was if he'd been hit by a bus. Blood soaked his face.

Poor old Harry was out of it, bounced like a doll off the mildewy wall, slumped down helpless in the gloom, like a rumpled shirt slipped from a hanger.

Homer came up the stairs three at a time. Thunder thunder thunder, his feet pounding. I slammed the door, locked it, flung the bed against it and the wardrobe. And a table.

I dived for the window, fumbled with the catch. Shit almighty, the damn thing was wedged tight! The catch came away in my hand. I threw a chair through it.

As the glass was still bouncing I scrambled on to the sill, paused hesitantly about the ten-feet fall, dropped into the yard as Homer disintegrated the door with his shoulder. I grabbed the chain securing my bike to a drainpipe, fiddled frantically to get the bloody key in. Jesus Christ! It broke suddenly and I ripped the chain out, threw the bike over the wall, vaulted awkwardly after, landed in a heap. I sprang uncannily up. Then I was off, pedalling down the alley like a mad thing, shouting to give myself encouragement.

I tore into the street, cranked off down towards Stratford. Going like the clappers. Pray God Harry's all right.

Homer launched himself in pursuit; there was no

145

need for me to look back to assure myself, I knew he was there. As surely as the sun pursues the moon.

But at least I was on wheels now, even if they were a bit unsteady. Click-click-click-click, I belted down a shallow hill, gaining on him with every yard. When I chanced a wobbly glance over my shoulder he was miles behind.

But you can't go downhill for ever. When the road began to rise, so Homer began cutting down my advantage; a pace at a time, a yard at a time. Until I could hear him breathing.

I pedalled furiously, though my thighs were tied in knots. And I sobbed for my futility.

Twenty minutes elapsed and still I drove my body on, just holding the bike out of his reach. I crested a brow, dropped out of Homer's sight for a moment so quickly turned off and headed north. Not a good idea. The street was full of lumber and rubble, women rocking prams between the potholes, grubby kids playing eyeballs along the trenches. I shouted like a madman as I sped amongst them. 'Get out the way! Get out the way!' They weren't pleased. One lout threw a lump of wood and nearly knocked me off.

Then the chain snapped and I crashed into a lamppost. So much for the bike. I picked myself up, darted into someone's house, past the amazed woman standing in her floral pinafore in the doorway. Down a passage, through the kitchen, through the yard, over a wall. This is terraced-house country, they grow like weeds all over the place. I was in a passageway between a thousand of them. And every one identical.

I heard a woman's scream as Homer came through after me.

I had climbed another wall by then, into somebody

else's yard. Their back door was locked so I kicked it out of the frame, beetled through a gloomy hallway, out into another by-road. Virtually the same as the last except that this was a bashful street and everyone had lace curtains up. All the mothers screamed in muted voices.

I did the same again, barging past a startled middle-aged woman, charging past her gormless husband cutting toenails on the kitchen table, flying over a wall.

Moments later I heard the scream signifying Homer's approach. Did the swine have no respect for people's privacy? I pelted off along the alley. I had snatched a bread knife from the last place. This might slow Homer up, I thought. But it probably wouldn't.

But where to now? I knew we were nearing the end of the chase; I'm only endowed with so much strength, and that had all been shed long ago. I only kept going at all because I still believe in miracles and the tooth fairy.

I stopped at the alley's end where a line of semi-slums turned its backside wall to me, and wondered which way to turn. I remember that, between the old wooden doors with their rattly latches, there were dozens of bluebottles, buzzing around the dustbins which had been set into the wall like grey fillings in a row of teeth.

Have you ever heard a bullet thwack into a dustbin? It goes thwang! Then it carries on through all the rubbish, out of the other side, across the yard and through someone's window into their living-room. If your gun's powerful enough that is.

Homer's gun was. The bang when he fired it nearly made my underpants fill, it was as if a plane had blown up. The echoes and re-echoes were almost enough to break all the windows.

I spun around, ready to surrender. I mean, let's face

147

it, when cannons go off you don't try outrunning them. Nor is there much point in brandishing your bread knife. Killers with cannons don't scare that easily.

It took but a glance down the forty odd yards to the hunter's face, to see that Homer hadn't punctured the dustbin accidentally. He had aimed there quite deliberately.

Homer was going to kill me. He wasn't going to let me give myself up. I could tell that from his stance, his patience, the rictus of his mouth.

The gun looked tiny in his huge pale hands. It looked for all the world like a guinea pig. Don't ask me how, it just looked as though he was offering me a sleek, black guinea pig. And I used to think they were cute.

When he fired again, I thought he had killed me. I saw the orange flash, heard the boom; my eyes snapped shut as if I was already dead, and the latch on a green door a couple of feet to my right pinged away.

Every organ in my body turned inside out when I head that report and when I opened my eyes I was dithering, my tongue was juddering against the roof of my mouth. Tears frosted my eyes. I had stopped inhaling, had to compel myself to release my nostrils. I half shouted something at the bastard Homer. I don't know what, it came out of its own accord. Then I wheeled to my left and jerked into horrified motion.

I knew, even as I lifted my first throbbing leg, that he wanted me to run. But what else could I do? I was shit scared.

Homer followed me right back to my home ground. Pushed me to the pit of absolute exhaustion.

It was really all up by then, my mind was all shot to

pieces. The only thought that kept me stumbling idiotically on was that if I stopped finally, Homer would kill me; but if I kept moving, I was still alive.

We'd been running for hours. It was late evening. Nobody intervened. I must have passed hundreds of people, they could see I was being tortured. But they didn't lift a finger. No one tried to find out what was going on.

I can't blame them I guess. I just don't like them for it.

Trouble is, according to the law of this glorious land of ours, I was in the wrong. And Homer, sadistic, inhuman, vicious bastard that he is, is the admirable God-blessed blameless hand of Right, the hero.

If I sound bitter, it's because I am. I didn't ask to join their bloody army. I don't ask them to put themselves out when I'm in trouble. Thanks a lot Britain. If ever you need anything from me, stuff it.

Life is so simple when you hold the gun. I hope they all rot in hell.

I realized that I was not far from home, not far from where this grisly episode began. At the end of the day, I hadn't moved at all. Is that what life's about? I was looking for a lair now. Somewhere to die in privacy.

Rows and rows of back-to-back gardenless terraces. And me a rat, hobbling through the fetid passageways which amputated blocks of dwellings. Wide passages, not generous enough to pass a car, but two men could walk without jostling. Not me, I bounced off the walls.

Listening to the echoes of my snorting breathing. Wondering who was mumbling; but it was only me. I could see the route dissolving into distance, alleyway, roadway, alleyway, roadway. A converging tunnel for ever. The eye of the vortex. As I emerged into one empty street a vehicle screeched and slewed around me. I'd nearly killed myself, didn't bother to look for traffic. You die one way, you die another. I didn't notice the little blue van that roared wildly.

I hobbled into the next vertiginous passage, looking back at the steady hunter as he closed with every alleyway we traversed. This was the end. I recognized it in his stride.

Perhaps he wanted to go home for his tea, I don't know. I heard a set of tyres screeching somewhere, like a horse in terror.

I left the gloom, crossed another bright street. At the bottom of the road I saw the blue van again, tearing towards me lickety-spit. But it was a long way off, it looked quite tiny. I limped into another tunnel.

I could see something ahead of me. A brown, lumpy object like a dead elephant across the path. It was a pile of boxes and cartons, blocking my way. I had almost reached the killing ground. At least I could lie down amongst the cardboard. I shook some of the water from my eyes, felt urine trickling down my leg.

Suddenly Harry appeared in front of me. Harry and Moose and another guy. All pointing guns at me. 'No!' I screamed.

'Get down, Beak!' Harry cried. 'Get down!' I heard him, but I didn't know what the hell he was saying. I just stood and looked at him, looked at all the purple blood masking half of his face. Regardless, they fired past me. Two light-machine guns and Harry's pistol blasted hell out of the murky air.

At the first crack I screamed, lost all control and fell on the ground thrashing and wailing like a mad thing. Which is probably how Homer came to shoot me in the foot.

Thank God I faint easily. The last thing I remember is Harry screaming wildly. And thunder. Good old Harry.

ELEVEN

A week has gone by and I'm still alive. Where are we now? Oh yeah, we're in an attic room in Leytonstone. The ceiling slopes and there are low pokey windows you have to kneel down to see from. It's like a wizard's den.

There's a hole in my foot where the blood seeps through. The doc says I'll always have a limp. But I'm okay.

What a waste hey? I get chased through London for hours and wind up shot in the foot. It hurts like hell. It feels as though I have a box of matches stuffed in there and somebody has just lit it. It keeps me awake at night. And sometimes it itches a lot.

It's really weird. What a business. Still, I've always wanted a limp.

It's nothing really. If you want to know what the major change in my life is, it's this: I sleep with a gun.

I have nightmares. And sudden noises frighten the willies out of me. For the first couple of days I was in a hell of a state.

They swear they hit Homer. They swear they hit him several times, in the chest, in the head, in the legs. They even showed me stains on the stones that look like blood.

But he scrambled over a wall and disappeared. How many times do you have to shoot someone before you kill them? Why didn't he just die?

Maybe he is dead. Maybe he died almost immediately. But nobody knows that. No one can *tell* me that.

Tommy made a few enquiries but learned nothing. It's as if the man just disappeared. Nobody can tell me that he's dead.

And so I have nightmares.

Harry's face isn't so bad now. It's still purple, and there's a bubbly scar about three inches long beneath his right eye. The skin pulled apart like the velvet on a ripe peach. But he's okay. He says they were driving around for ages looking for me. They were on their way home when I ran in front of them.

Don't try telling me there are no miracles and no tooth fairies.

So, for the present, I'm just resting up, taking it easy. I hear that a record seven out of ten of the working population is now out of work. Judging by the din coming from the little park opposite, most of them are just outside.

This hot weather brings them out like maggots on a corpse. Seven out of ten. That's bloody ludicrous. And this is while there's a war on, what would we be like in peacetime? Whatever happened to the government's education programme?

It's no bloody wonder that fell through. Who the hell wants to learn oil painting or Sanskrit?

Gorblimey, they couldn't teach a hen to lay an egg.

I've not seen a great deal of Harry in the last couple of days; another job is coming up and he's pretty involved running things about. He figures it's going to be a heist.

I don't know if I'm included. I don't know whether I want to be. I'd like to clear my 'obligation', get the hell out of here. But I couldn't go through something like that Fitzwilliam affair again.

For now I'm just going to lie here and contemplate the hole in my foot.

TWELVE

Nothing to report for the last couple of weeks, it's been a very quiet time. If you knew what had been happening to me during the last couple of weeks, you'd be glad you missed it. Boredom man, with a capital B.

Nationally it's been a fairly interesting time. Riots in Nottingham and Liverpool, a national strike last Wednesday, and the one before, a remarkably accurate sniper attack on the parliament buildings, the suicide of pop heart-throb Slit Tyger by disembowelment.

The disembowelling of Slit was unusual; the damn fool videoed it and Channel Five put it out last night. Talk about nauseating, the guy had only just had his dinner.

Last evening there was a tactical discussion of the heist which goes down next week.

Hell's teeth man, this is a big job. Six vans, two cars, twenty-four men, eight women, four bazookas, eight light-machine guns, twelve shotguns, six Steyrs, thirty-two pistols, three hundred pounds of explosive, grenades, gas, gas masks, acid, back-up squads – it's like a commando force preparing to take Crete. I felt like a kid at a grown-ups' party.

The actual target is the post office building in Whitechapel Road. I know that place. I had to go there once to prove my identity. And they didn't bloody believe me then, I could see it in the guy's glass eyes.

They weren't real glass, they just looked as if they were made of glass, cold, shiny, aiming in different directions. He was an ignoramus.

Thankfully my role in this major event is a relatively minor one. I'm reserve driver for one of the vans (they must be out of their minds) and I'm to blast off with a pump shotgun at any faces that appear at windows. A pump shotgun. Sounds like I'm shooting farts at the poor buggers.

THIRTEEN

Tomorrow evening the job goes down.

Final preparations. Like saying my prayers (Dear God, please don't let me die tomorrow) and taking an overnight laxative.

My foot is much better now. So long as I don't have to stamp on anyone's head I'll be all right. But it's just as well those vans are automatic, it's not wise to be tearing away from the scene of a crime stuck in first gear.

This job though has developed sinister overtones. Perhaps not the job so much, but the people I'm involved with. I think they're a bunch of quislings. The rotten snakes in the grass.

Harry thinks that after the job, I'm going to be exchanged for an imprisoned NDP lieutenant.

It is not what I understood our arrangement to be. This, as I understand it, is called 'selling down the line'. And it doesn't thrill me one little bit. The lousy Judases.

In strictly ethical terms, such a practice might be deemed underhand, perfidious and snide. But we are not dealing in strictly ethical matters; we are dealing with people. A promise made is a promise betrayed.

Not unnaturally, since they know he's my buddy, nobody has come up to Harry to say: 'Hey Hal, we're selling your pal Beekay down the line. Got a guy over at Police Central who's willing to do a deal.'

But quiet Harry notices things. A lot of quiet people are like that, they hear things in the silences, like madmen. He may be illiterate, but Harry's no fool. He has suspicions. And he says it is just the kind of dirty, malfeasant, cheapskate trick they'd perform. Actually he didn't say malfeasant, he said cockfarty.

He's warned me to beware.

Believe me, I'm bewaring for all I'm worth.

FOURTEEN

Evening, nine forty-five, I'm squashed in a van with four thugs I've never seen before. They're big, big as bloody Titans. I mean, I'm not small myself, but these guys make me look like Pinocchio. I wouldn't like to be a mattress under any of them.

We had kind of vaguely introduced ourselves, but the only one I can remember is the driver, called Declan.

What a scorcher today has been. I look like an incensed lobster. Even my eyeballs have a tan and my nose is throbbing like a beacon.

The evening is just as hot. Hotter. The smell of sweat in the crowded vehicle is overpowering. And my hay fever is crippling me. It's coming out of my ears. And it's all Harry's fault, the clod-footed lout trod on my inhaler. Even now the sky is still boiling and looks ready to burst out in some pustular disease.

We are in a small siding off the Whitechapel Road, about a quarter of a mile, Aldgate way, from the post office. Been here nearly half an hour, breathing in each other's smell. And cigarette smoke. There is so much smoke we have to keep getting out to see if anything is going on.

It all seems very suspicious to me, but nobody's taking any notice of us. I'm probably just too sensitive.

There is a face lying in my lap, and it keeps looking at

me curiously. It's a face mask, we all wear them for the robbery. I'm Spiderman. Next to me is Frankenstein's monster. Behind us are two little piggies and a frog. They look bloody stupid. Their heads are so big the masks only cover the middle of their faces. They keep trying them on and falling about laughing like idiots. I wouldn't be surprised if they wet themselves in a minute. Come to that, I wouldn't be surprised if I did. My stomach is being liquidized.

Frankenstein's monster keeps farting. This is the kind of company I keep nowadays. Lord, what would my mother say; I don't think she ever farted in her life. She probably just hissed, the way some dogs do.

I look at Declan's watch again. Nine forty-seven. At nine-fifty we should know whether the caper is on or off. It's dependent on other things, if they cock-up it's all off and we go home.

We are all tense, waiting for the word. There's a lot of money at stake. Friday night, the post office is a reservoir for the whole area, money pours in from all over the place. Great if you like water, but I've never been able to swim. I hope we don't fall in. At nine-fifty on the button the walkie-talkie speaks to us.

'The hare is off and running.' They're very punctual, I'll say that for them.

There is a great sigh of relief and the tension crackles. We crack a few devastatingly unfunny jokes and the frog goes hysterical.

Inside the post office the tapestry is almost complete. The monies will all have been counted and bagged and packed into square steel boxes. The boxes will be on their way to a loading bay where two yellow armoured carriers await, and a team of men under the supervision of a dozen armed guards will begin to load.

At ten-fifteen a small military convoy will roll up from the direction of Shoreditch. The two armed guards outside the steel-doored bay will pass the word, and the armoured carriers will join the procession. Then the whole kit and caboodle will trundle off to Chancery Lane where the boxes will be entrusted to an impenetrable stygian vault where the world ends. And there they will stay until some paunchy bigshot wants to spend them.

The value of the boxes averages two and a half million pounds. Enough to buy you shade dark-brown suntans for the rest of your life, and some. Sometimes it's as much as four million. Sometimes only two. We're not greedy, we'll settle for two. I'd settle for twenty quid.

In the fifteen minutes between the arrival of the money boxes in the bay and the arrival of the military convoy we have to remove them. It's as simple and monumental as that. Only about a thousand and one things can go wrong. At least, that's how many I've counted in the last couple of days.

My conscience though is clear. Stealing money is all right. If it is the government's money, so much the better. I don't intend killing anybody.

Besides, my conscience hasn't the bull to muscle in on the turmoil of thoughts which roil behind my ridiculous Spiderman mask. For the coming adventure isn't the only thing on my mind. I have a little plan of my own.

If my nerve holds out.

At a little before ten, two girls stroll around a street corner and make towards the post office building. The evening is quite blue now, a few lights are on, sparkling like eyes in the dusk.

The street is wide, with broad grey pavements trimmed with shops and taverns. Twixt us and the post office is a hospital, dark-stoned and brooding, its many lights soft and yellow throughout the high Victorian walls. A few people are promenading, not many, but enough to give life to the scene. Some filter out of the underground station, between the hospital and the post office, on the opposite side of the road. There is no traffic; temporary yellow and black barricades have been set up to keep the way clear for the convoy.

The two girls are laughing and fooling about. They look cute in tight jeans and check shirts with their hair all tousled and wild. They sport matching yellow shoulder bags.

We can just about see them from where we sit, through a tear in some old hoarding. We watch as they approach the sentries. Declan fires the engine and lets it idle. The van chunters quietly to itself.

The girls hang around the guards being cheeky. The guards, being guards, are very cool and macho. There is a clash of interests.

But the girls are fun, they persist in hanging around, and the guards are only human. Well, almost human. They relax a smidgin. The pretty girls sidle closer, a beguiling mixture, teasing and brazen. They finger the guards' heavy stens, they pout their shiny lipstick.

A touch before ten there is a boom over to the west, another behind us. Dull explosions, muffled and visceral. If you weren't expecting them you might not even notice, they could pass for kids tossing gas canisters on to bonfires.

The telephones in the area are now out of action. The

local exchanges have been taken over and blown. In another minute the power supply should go.

The traps are open.

If the two guards hear the concurrent rumbles they do not notice. The girls mince behind them, joking gaily. It is just on the point of ten. From the yellow shoulder bags two revolvers are produced. The girls camly press them into the sentries' necks, blast their silent brains out as simply as capping eggs. The guards buck forward a yard as the heavy slugs lift them, collapse like a pair of lightning-struck trees. Their brains bubble out.

The dogs are running. We lurch forward, squeal into the road. Already the girls are running to clear the barricades, pulling them aside in an urgent clatter. We charge through, roar towards the target.

At the same moment three vans screech from the other direction. They spread out in front of the post office. We stop about forty yards short, spill out, take cover behind the vehicle. Someone hands me a shot-gun.

A brown van races past me, shrieks to a halt two or three hundred yards up the road. A boy springs out, lays a line of antenna-mines from shopfront to shopfront, a few feet apart, leaps back into the van. Already a similar line of mines has been strung out a quarter of a mile in the other direction.

These mines respond to the vibration of vehicles or the physical movement of the boxes themselves. They are all digitally tuned in to a master control and they're buggers to defuse. It's like a combination, once it's set there could be a million solutions. They look like bright blue bread bins, with a twelve-inch white aeriel sticking from the top of each.

When the brown van has cleared out of the way the mines are activated. Now anything coming within five yards will be blown into the next world. At least they'll arrive with a bang.

While all that's going on two guys in Balaclavas slap a couple of hundred pounds of explosive against the steel doors. We all cram ear-mufflers on. It's half a minute after ten.

Detonators are set. And with a suddenness that makes your heart jump every light in the vicinity goes out. The sub-stations have been blown.

We take cover and the doors blow up like a quarry face. A tremendous bang, hundreds of panes of glass in scores of windows buckle inwards and fulminate; the wave of concussion numbs our teeth and makes the road vibrate for a dozen seconds.

We cradle our heads as lumps of stone and brick clatter down and nuggets of dripping steel bounce angrily along the tarmac like enraged bees from a smoking hive. There is a lot of shouting as people round about realize something is going on. They're very observant in these parts.

Blinding spotlights flood into the loading bay and I glimpse the bonnet of the first armoured carrier. Someone lobs a couple of gas canisters in and orange smoke fizzes out madly.

Sub-machine guns open up within the bay and the fleeing negro girl who lobbed the gas is ripped apart; I see chunks of her fly off in all directions and her head falls off.

The salvo is returned, bullets and grenades pour into the building. The whole of the recess seems to be on fire. But somehow the guards within keep blasting away.

The din is appalling, it roars and rants and bounds, rebounds, until you can no longer think; so dreadfully loud that it's almost blinding. I press into the side of the van in a perverse embrace. I can hear a big gun thudding down the street, dumpa-dumpa-dumpa, it pours what look like streaky balls of fire into blazing upstairs windows. It's like a bloody war. I begin to scream, I can't help it.

Faces appear at windows on the second storey and someone yells at me to blast them. I jerk up, aim high, blast a few chunks out of the dark, empty third floor, but the faces wisely disappear.

I see a few mugs in windows across the street, so pump a couple into the air to frighten them away.

The battle for the bay still rages. Men in masks are edging forward, converging inexorably on the blazing maw, crawling on their bellies along the gutters. More gas canisters skitter in. You can hardly see anything for smoke now. It's like the boiler-room of hell.

The spotlights wave back and forth across the façade like tentacles seeking a hold. A grenade goes off in somebody's hand and sends a man screaming, armless, into the line of fire, where he suddenly becomes a rag doll, jerking dementedly, spewing out his stuffing.

I suddenly realize that somebody is firing at me. I'd thought I was out of it all over here. But sudden holes are splatting like snowballs into the roof of the van. I look up and a pale, bespectacled guy with the face of an angry dog is aiming a rifle from the second storey that I reprieved. I pop my gun over the roof, pump a couple of rounds in his direction and a look of terror freezes on his features an instant before he scuttles out of sight. And don't come back! I cry.

The orange gas has taken effect now. The loading

bay is suddenly, ominously quiet. Two cumbersome figures run forward, eerily garbed in gas masks and silver suits. There's not much in there for fire to flourish on, they kill the flames in seconds with pressure extinguishers, and drag a couple of blackened bodies out of the doorway.

In the abrupt silence of the street every sound seems embarrassed and posed. But up above fire is devouring the smokey heights of the grey building and people are on the roof screaming. I try to ignore it, concentrate on what's going down on the ground.

Amazingly, only a couple of minutes have elapsed; I can see a clock on the post office wall and it isn't five past ten yet.

A group of men runs forward, rattling along behind shopping trolleys. It looks like some crazy village hall race, except that they're all wearing gas masks. There must be a dozen of them. They clip-clop through the spotlights into the smoking, ravaged bay. And we outside wait tensely, chary of the pregnant calm. We count off seconds as if they are prison sentences.

Then the first man appears, his trolley creaking under the weight of two of the monetary coffins. The second man is right behind, close on the toes of the third. They clatter out into the street.

Some of us stand up, fascinated by these metal carriers, allured by the Circe within.

We watch spellbound as the skeletal carts trundle towards us, rickety and flimsy and laden with loot. I help load a couple into the van. The paint on them has blistered off.

Then back the gas-proof men go for more.

We wait in the silent street like shy, distant mourners around a burial. It is dark now, save for the white, bright lights and the red glow overhead. There is a strange muteness about us all.

I am so fascinated by the proceedings that I almost forget what I have in mind. It's getting near the time.

Soon there are six money boxes in the back of the van. The operation has been executed beautifully. I look at Declan who is leaning on the open driver's door, his huge back trustingly towards me. The two piggies and the frog are off elsewhere, loading maybe or planting diversionary incendiaries around the back of the hospital so that as much chaos as possible confuses our escape. Elsewhere a fire station, a plastics warehouse and a distillery are being ignited.

I look around. We must be fifty yards from anyone else. I swallow my heart. Suddenly I reverse the shotgun in my hands, and clout Frankenstein's monster a mighty blow on the back of the head. He goes down like a man made up of spare parts. I drag him away from the door.

There's not much time to lose now, my life is fluttering in a web. I slam the rear doors of the van, tumble into the driving seat, put the shotgun by my side. I goad the engine, stamp on the pedal, swing the bonnet through the tightest arc.

As I bounce up and off the opposite pavement I catch a glimpse of a lone dark figure hurtling like a whippet down the road towards me. At the same time a voice cries desperately, 'Wait for me, Beak! Wait for me!' It's Harry.

I jerk up, he flings open the passenger door, dives beside me.

'Go Beak go!' he cries, and we roar off whooping.

*

Two hundred yards from a line of delicate antenna-mines and I suddenly realized this was as far as my thinking had got.

There were no turnings, we had to go through or go back, and the bloody van was roaring to get there. 'What'll we do?' I screamed. 'Shoot the mines?'

'Bollocks!' Harry cried. 'Ye'll send us to kingdom come!' Suddenly he leaned over me, rammed his foot over mine on the drive pedal and banged down hard. 'Drive ye madman, bloody drive!' The van sprang forward.

'What are you doing?' I screamed. 'You'll blow us to bits!' That's all I needed, a bloody lunatic beside me.

'Go on! Go on!' cried Harry as the motor opened up and accelerated us towards a certain demise. I mean, even though we're the good guys, those bread bins just aren't selective. And we're not that good anyway.

At forty miles an hour and still climbing we were forty yards from doom. Another thirty and we'd hit the angels. I was blank with panic. This wasn't what I'd had in mind at all. Trust the bloody Irish to get it wrong.

Harry had tight hold of the wheel, as solid as a rock. He was panting like a runner, I've never seen a face look so determined, so intent. Pity he was about to have it blown off.

Suddenly he wrenched the wheel out of my terrified hands and swung the van hard over. We bounced off a kerb, plunged through the black, stickered window of a long-abandoned shop.

'Aiyeeee!' That was me screaming.

Smack! A glassy supernova showered spectacularly into the aphotic void. Crunch, the back wheels hit the ground.

We bounced off the floor of a deserted health food

store, thunked through a partition wall at the back and crashed straight through a brick wall into an empty yard taking an old steel sink with us.

The van was bucking and screaming like a mad thing. Much like myself.

We'd lost most of the speed now, by the time we careered into the wall at the foot of the yard we'd enough momentum to punch a hole but not enough to break through. A lambrequin of bricks stopped a couple of inches from the windscreen and the tip of my nose, and the engine wailed.

What a shroud of disappointment fell over me then. For one glorious, tantalizing, terrifying moment, I'd thought we were going to get away with it. Now it was all over, shot down in flames before it ever really got off the ground.

I think that I must never have felt so sad. I believe I wanted to cry.

But Harry hadn't finished yet. He dragged me out of the seat. 'Move over Beak! Come on, it's not over yet!' He clambered over me, his slight body hard as a wooden doll, knocked the stick into reverse, bumped us back a couple of yards.

Then we rammed forward, the engine snarling dementedly. We knocked a few dusty bricks out. Back again, another few feet of acceleration. Bang! we hit the wall once more. We weren't so much driving through as climbing over it, the plucky little van was scrambling and juddering as it clawed at the heap of rubble, muttering and chittering in the way a dog worries a stick.

I looked out of the rear window. Nobody in sight yet. We lurched back again, gave the van another run. Bumph! we bounced on to the brick hurdle, skittered and slewed as the front wheels scrabbled for purchase. We tottered up another yard, halfway through the opening now. Slid back protesting. Harry was screaming furiously. 'Up you bastard! Go on you damn car!' Honestly, his language is appalling at times.

I grabbed a gun in case anyone came on us.

Again we battered forward, jolted over the reluctant, stubborn, bloody rampart, nosed despairingly into the beckoning night beyond. I didn't know whether to look before or behind.

'Harry!' I yelled. 'Harry!' I'm a lot of good in a crisis.

'Get out!' he cried. 'Push the bugger!'

We tumbled out, Harry wedged the pedal down with a brick and we huffed and puffed and grunted at the doors, half dragging, half shoving the screeching van over the demolition and out into the night.

All of a sudden we were through. The vehicle was sliding and pawing into the dark regions beyond. We dived back in, Harry threw the brick out and with a squeal of triumphant rubber the van charged victoriously away.

I couldn't believe it. There we were, bouncing and careening across a wide expanse of cleared ground, swerving around potholes and ruts and bounding over mounds.

I looked back. We were entirely alone. There was no sign of anybody. We'd done it. We'd bloody done it!

I looked at Harry. And he looked at me. And all at once we were laughing like idiots. We were rolling about on the seats like a couple of kids.

We nearly killed ourselves, we were laughing so much. Harry all but drove into an uncovered cellar. He stopped about two inches short. It was hysterical! We shrieked with glee as the van backed up and roared off in another direction. We swerved on to a road, headed north and finally managed to stop laughing.

'What's in the back?' asked Harry as he eased off on the accelerator.

I checked in the gloom. 'Six boxes. How much is that?'

Harry reckoned up, moving his lips wordlessly. It seemed to take about ten minutes. Then he said: 'One hundred and eighty thousand pounds. Jesus Christ, Beekay, we've got nearly two hundred grand!' We fell about again and the grin on Harry's face threatened to split his head in two.

Seeing it reminded me to pull my Spiderman mask off.

'America?' I asked him soberly.

And Harry thought about it a while before replying. Then he nodded once, determinedly. 'Yeah,' he said. 'America.'

The van screeched to a halt outside the Alhambra cafeteria and Harry switched off the engine.

We sat there silently for a minute, looking ahead, panting. Then Harry looked at me.

'Go on,' I urged. 'Go and ask her.'

He screwed his face up. 'You ask her,' he said. 'Go on, you go.'

'No go on, all you have to do is ask her.'

Harry's face continued to writhe. 'I don't like to. I'm shy. She might laugh.'

'She won't laugh.' But I could see he'd lost his nerve. I sighed. 'All right, I'll ask her. But it's not my fault if she says no.'

I jumped out of the van, dashed into the ill-lit

Alhambra with its plastic coffee and its sugar-sprinkled tables, and blinked at the din from the scratchy stereo on the counter. I banged the door shut, and squinted through the smoky interior.

The place was virtually empty; a couple of homos holding hands under a tattered Jimmy Dean poster; a young, jaundiced, introspective-looking chick with tracks of mascara following gooey tears down her inflamed acne; a couple of knackered hookers rolling thin joints.

Rachel, looking sleepy, was at a corner table blinking at some weedy little guy who should have been home with his wife and who looked decidedly uncomfortable in his surroundings.

I dashed up to her, grabbed her hand. ''Scuse me,' I said to the weed, 'I won't be a minute.' He looked nonplussed and Raych shrugged. She tagged along as I led her arm away. I paused by the door to have a look at the new purple bracelet on her wrist. 'Nice,' I said. 'Looks like real plastic.' We bundled outside.

'That's the way to treat 'em Beak,' she said. 'Be manly. You looking for a good time?'

'Not now you bloody whore,' I said and I grabbed her hands in mine. Fortunately she only had two.

'Listen Raych, we've just robbed a hundred and eighty thousand pounds.' I paused a moment for dramatic impact. 'We're going for Gay. D'you want to come to America with us?'

'America?' She was a bit confused. 'America? Who with?'

'Harry. Harry and me.'

'Harry?' She showed a little cautious interest. 'Me and Harry? Go to America?'

'Yeah, all of us. The four of us. We're going to hire a cabin.'

'Harry wants me to go to America with him?' She frowned unconfidently. 'Are you sure you've got that right? I mean, are you sure he means me?'

'Of course he bloody means you. Look,' I pointed at the van, 'ask him yourself.'

She looked at Harry's embarrassed, pale face, smiling hopefully through the open window and he waved stupidly.

'Do you want me to?'

Harry nodded. 'If you'd like to. Only if you want to. I mean, I want you to – but not if you don't. If you don't want to. . . .'

They looked at each other.

I stood there like a bloody prick, waiting for something to happen, watching those two prunes fidget like idiots.

'Are you sure?' she asked him again.

'Goddammit of course he's bloody sure!' I cried. 'Otherwise we wouldn't bloody be here would we!'

Rachel looked at me, struggling to fight the reluctance within her. Frightened. 'The four of us? You're not joking are you?'

I shook my head. 'No,' I said quietly, 'it's not a joke. The four of us. Do you want to come?'

'Er – er . . .' she looked at Harry, looked at the Alhambra, back to Harry, back to the Alhambra, looked at me. This could go on all night. 'You bet your sweet life I do,' she grinned.

'Then for Christ's sake get in!' I screamed.

Over her shoulder I saw Harry smiling fit to bust and I winked. What a pair of softies.

FIFTEEN

It's a sunny morning and we merry band of three are on
the outskirts of Leighton Buzzard.

Don't ask me to explain how we got here; none of us
knew the way so we just kind of drove around until we
found the place. We ended up in Aylesbury three times.
That's not much of a place I can tell you. If you're
planning a holiday, don't go there.

We're lying on our bellies on a flat hilltop, basking in
the midges. The sun is behind us, beating on our bare
shoulders, and above, a rank of spidery trees occasionally
leans over to dapple us with mollifying ghosts. A
skylark sings, or is it a blackbird? A little green thing
crawls over my anaemic fingernails.

Harry and Rachel are playing footsy and silly
buggars and I have to be firm with them. As usual they
take no notice, and Rachel pokes a piece of grass into
my ear. Youth! I snort.

I take up the field glasses and review the scene again,
for the umpteenth time. That's one thing about lifting a
van that's been used for a well-armed robbery, you get
a load of gear with it. We have grenades, gas, a light-
machine gun, two pistols, a bag of tools, a pair of field
glasses, and nearly two hundred thousand pounds. We
even have one of the new Steyrs; a great gun that if you
like killing people, it does everything but strangle
them.

I hope, sincerely, that we do not have to shoot anybody. I hope we don't even have to shout at them. I've seen enough violence.

I fiddle the eyepiece into focus.

The hill slopes easily away beneath its pelt of grass and we can see a long way in three directions. The sky is like an ocean, with the sun reflected in it; it is watery, with high, white-horse clouds and a rippling haze.

Six hundred yards away, at the foot of the hill, a redbrick factory stands and muses. The only thing between it and us is a high perimeter fence and a thin field fence.

This is the sail factory where Gay slaves. Coming from the right a road passes in front of the great edifice and continues on northwards through Leighton Buzzard, dropping tributaries into the town like parasitic worms. On the far side of the road from the factory there is a large, fenced enclosure, a compound, where a cluster of low, grey, concrete constructions nestles, looking like a barracks. This is the camp for the women. It is patrolled by dogs and men with big feet. From the enclosure gate to the factory gate is about fifty yards.

There is a gap of half a mile between these two places and the start of the town proper. But on the nearer side there are two neat terraces of staff homes and shops like a village street and a couple of blocks of two-storey flats beyond. There is also, on the farther side, a sewage plant.

A mile to our left, which is northeast, we can see construction of the Canal under way. A great rift has been hewn out of the land and the landscape is pocked by barrows of earth and rock, by blankets of concrete dust, machinery, billets, lorries and groups of men like

174

grey amoeba. Even from here the *brouhaha* is plain. And the air above cradles a sluggish cloud of terracotta dust and smoke, which gradually precipitates over all the land around, so that only because of the night's heavy showers is the hillside green again.

I see some activity through the glasses. 'Where's the pencil?' I ask.

'Behind my ear,' responds Harry. 'Who's got the paper?'

'I'm lying on it,' says Rachel.

'Why have you got the pencil when you can't write?' I snatch it off him, write down: '10.24: lorry arrives to empty bins.'

'I still like the first plan,' says Harry. 'Drive in with all guns blazing.'

'This isn't a bloody movie. In real life you get shot to pieces when you try stunts like that.'

'Yeah. But it'd be exciting wouldn't it?'

I think the guy's brain has gone on vacation.

SIXTEEN

It was raining when I stood at a window and watched Rachel this morning. Not a lot but enough to speckle the ground with silver and keep the pollen down. The sort of day to look for rainbows.

As soon as I saw her I thought, this is crazy, this will never work. We've been reading too many comics. We must be out of our minds.

But by then of course, as always, it was too late. She was already inside, and the wheel was spinning. I looked to the sky, hoping for a bit of magic. But not a rainbow in sight. Just the sparkling rain.

The gods were against us.

We must have been out of our minds. Crackers to think we could get away with it. It didn't need the gods to thwart us, the plan itself was stupid from the start. It only works in movies. You can't get away with harebrained schemes in real life. We practically begged to be caught.

I shuddered as I stood at a window and watched Rachel this morning.

She walked between the high, steel-mesh gates and flashed her little green pass as if she'd worked in the place for years. As she slouched in a queue to go through the metal scanner she spat out her gum, poked half a ciggy between her lips and cadged a light from the girl behind. She looked a natural.

I watched her waiting for the urns to come out of the van, standing nonchalantly, her hair tied up in a blue cap. She saw me, but didn't crack on. Nor did I.

It was just before noon. And we were both inside the prison-factory compound.

Like I said, we must have been out of our bloody minds.

Raych was wearing the blue and orange uniform of one of the civilian domestics who come from Leighton Buzzard with the meal vans. More specifically, she was wearing the outfit of the young gozzy-eyed chick who serves the tea at lunchtime.

The gozzy-eyed kid had gone to the big L for the day, with two hundred of our ill-gained smackers itching in her purse. Harry had even put her on the train, to make sure she went. But if anybody asks, poor gozzy-eyes is very poorly. She was lucky to have her cousin Rachel able to stand in for her at such short notice.

I hoped that anybody we came into contact with was as stupid and gullible as that bloody plan of ours. We must have been smashed out of our brains when we cooked that little lot up! If I remember rightly, we were.

I was there as the nephew of the caretaker and I walked around in blue dungarees carrying a tool bag.

The real caretaker wasn't tempted by the fistful of good-time we wafted under his nose. So he had been tied up in the back of the van overnight. I hope he didn't want to go to the toilet, the way he was gagged Harry probably wouldn't have heard him.

God, it was a long day. I'd been there since eight

177

o'clock and it was only noon then. I could hardly keep my eyes open.

Still, if all went well, we wouldn't be there much longer. No, we'd probably be dead. Or locked up in a prison van.

My God, if the scheme worked, we deserved to get away with it. Let's face it, none of us are heroes. Yet there we were, walking into the lion's den like little Daniels all.

I've always thought the Bible is a load of fairy tales.

The six urns were unloaded from the canteen van and Rachel wheeled them, one at a time, into the prison refectory.

I went to the janitor's room to wait. I drummed my fingers. I paced up and down. I smoked four cigarettes in ten minutes and burned my mouth.

At twelve-fifteen I heard footsteps outside and busied myself with a screwdriver and a little thingummy lying on the workbench. It should have been Rachel, but I didn't take any chances.

The door swung open, and my stomach flipped. It was one of the warders. A big one. Eight feet tall and still growing.

'Where's Dago?'

'He's sick,' I said faintly. 'I'm his nephew.'

'Oh. Well I've got one of the tea urns here. The girl said it ain't workin' right. Maybe it's the plug.'

'Oh, right, I'll have a look at it then.' Jesus H., Rachel, you were supposed to wheel it over yourself.

'If you have a look now I'll take it back for you.'

Just what I didn't need. The thing was full of

grenades and gas. Assuming Rachel had managed to plant it. 'It's okay, I'll take it myself.'

'Nah, nothin' else to do.' He sat down on Dago's stool and swung his feet up on to the bench. 'Are you his sister Pamela's kid?'

'Yeah, that's right.' I started dismantling the plug.

'How is she now?'

I hadn't the faintest bloody idea. 'Oh, you know,' I shrugged.

'Yeah.' He picked his teeth out with a rusty nail. 'I knew a bloke who had just the same thing. Operated on him four times they did, before he died.'

Well, that limited the possibilities a little. It couldn't be cervical cancer or swollen ovaries. Could it?

'Course, I don't trust them friggin' doctors as far as I can throw 'em, know what I mean? I mean, you don't know you've got what they say you've got, do you?'

'That's true.' And a pretty pointless thing to say. I put the plug together again.

'I mean, like, if they say you've got a ruptured hernia, you just take their word for it, don't you?'

'I guess so.'

'D'you see what I'm gettin' at?'

'Oh yeah.' Why don't you drop dead you cretin? 'It's not the plug. Must be the connections.' I took the lid off, had a look inside. There it was, all wrapped up in PVC, floating in tea.

'See, I know a bloke who went in with a weak bladder and they took both his legs off.'

'Maybe they sprang a leak,' I muttered. How to get the stuff out, without this fount of sagacity observing all, that was the problem.

'*And* they never fixed his bladder.'

I could either slug him, and take the chance, with

179

only half an hour to go. Or I could distract him. How?

'My bladder's not bloody right itself you know. My missus says it's all the tea I drink. I drink a lot of tea.'

'Could you do us a favour?'

'Yeah, sure.'

'Could you go back and ask the girl whether she's adjusted the sprocket modulator, cos if she has, this thing's jiggered.'

'The sprocket modulator?' The screw frowned. 'Right. I'll just be two ticks.' He adjusted the crutch of his trousers, went out.

I hauled the dripping parcel out, stashed it behind a crate. Then I topped up the urn with a bucket of water from the permanently hissing tap on the wall. Some poor buggers were going to have a weak brew today.

A minute later the bozo returned. 'She says she's never heard of it. And even if she had fiddled with it, it's none of my bleedin' business.' That sounds like Rachel.

'It's okay, I think I've fixed it now.'

'Right. I'll see you later then.'

I bloody hope not.

'What's your name by the way?'

'Damian.' Damian?

'See you later then Damian.'

'Yeah. So long.'

Twelve-fifteen found me on the first floor, looking down and across the canteen from a grimy, fly-speckled window. I was planning to make my moves in a few minutes but I stole time to take a look at Gay.

It took me a while to pick her out of the hundreds of other grey milling uniforms. It was like a cattle

180

auction. God, why do they treat people like that?

Poor Gay, even from behind she looked rough. Grey, her hair losing shape, losing colour. Her hands red and rough. She looked scrawny, like a spring bird. It wasn't right.

Gay couldn't believe her eyes. But Rachel was as calm as a nun, though her cheeks were flushed. She'd had half a bottle of whisky before she went in. She was chatting with Gay, the way she'd chatted with a few of the other prisoners.

It was one-sided though, for Gay was speechless. Her hands were trembling. She looked terrified.

I found out later what Raych was saying to her.

'You'll be glad of a break I expect,' as she wiped out a cup with a nearly clean cloth.

She started filling the cup from a trickling spout. 'I bet you're looking forward to getting out of here – seeing your boyfriend again.' She glanced up at me as she said that, and Gay, following her gaze, nearly choked.

'Course, you'll have a while to wait yet I expect,' said Rachel, distracting her. She looked at the big white wall clock. 'Gor, I'll be glad to knock off today. Another half hour or so, then we can go home.'

Gay nearly dropped her cup as she took it from Rachel. As it was she spilled most of it on the way to her seat.

I took a deep breath and left the window, resolved.

Clutching the heavy bag of tools I went first to the screws' rest-room. I was pretty familiar with the layout of the factory now, having spent most of the morning wandering innocently around with a mop and a bucket.

I looked inside. It was almost empty, so I walked in.

181

It wasn't a large room, about twenty feet by ten. Everything was grey or green plastic, the ceiling, the tables, the chairs, the sandwich dispenser, the sandwiches.

Four screws were shuffling cards over a table by the counter, and a griseous old dame was poring over a crossword. I walked across the room to the juke box. 'Oi oi!' called one of the screws. I grinned and nodded. Prat.

I pulled the machine away from the wall and unplugged it.

'Something wrong with it?' They're really quick these guys.

'Faulty plug,' I called over my shoulder. 'Dago asked me to change it.'

I crouched down, my back to most of the room, and flopped open the bag. I went through the motions of changing the plug, and when a quick glance revealed that everyone's attention was elsewhere I whipped out a yellow cylinder and stuck it behind the machine. It was a canister of nerve gas. It wouldn't do anybody permanent harm, but in a couple of minutes everyone in the room would be out cold, and anyone entering would last for about one deep breath.

I stuck the plug back in the socket, pulled the machine up to the wall, and at the last second took a good breath and peeled off the tape which released the gas. It's colourless and odourless, but hisses as it comes out; so to hide the hiss I put a couple of coins in the juke, pressed a few buttons.

'Thanks Jimmy,' said one of the screws as the music bubbled out. 'Wanna join us for a game?'

I shook a rueful head. 'Can't I'm sorry. I've got a break-out to organize.' They all laughed.

I went next door to the screws' bog. God, what a stink. They sure didn't keep themselves too clean these guys. I put another yellow canister in one of the cisterns, pulled the tab off, flushed the loo, went away to continue my nefarious business, feeling a bit like a naughty boy up to pranks.

I checked the time. Almost twelve-thirty; Harry should have been pulling up the van a little way from the gates, lifting the bonnet, fiddling around as if the engine was on the blink. But not too close, we didn't want to alert suspicion.

I went back to the janitor's room, collected a can of paraffin, and went next to the store-room on the first floor, where a chute feeds the loading bay with bales of prepared, dyed cloth. It was deserted, there were just bolts of white and red cloth standing about looking lonely, waiting to be incinerated. My heart was thumping, my back was sticky with sweat.

I closed the door, strewed the cloth around until there was a big pile of it just inside. I set two of Harry's homemade incendiaries in the heap, splashed the paraffin about quietly and buggered off. They should ignite in three minutes.

I hurried downstairs. I could hardly breathe by then, the tension in my chest was suffocating. My legs were wobbling. I went down to the boiler-room, counting seconds as I went.

When I reached two hundred and fifty, I took the grenades out of my bag. There were two with green buttons and two with red. Oh God, my mind went blank, which was which? Two of them had thirty-second fuses, two only waited for six. Which was it?

And all the time, the back of my mind kept ticking off the moments. The store-room, with the open chute to fan the flames, should have been ablaze by then.

I remembered – red for danger, chuck it and run. I stuffed them into my left-hand pocket, put the two green ones in the right.

There was a big oil tank on the wall, it would hold about forty gallons when it was full. It was half empty now. But not for long. I turned the release tap and let it spill down on to the floor.

The count had reached four-fifty. I went back upstairs.

I could smell smoke before I reached the passageway leading to the store-room. When I turned the next corner I saw the door alight and flames already licking towards the ceiling. Great!

I waited another couple of minutes, until the blaze had snaked into the corridor and the floor was well alight. Then I turned and ran. 'Fire!' I screamed. 'Fire!' I banged an alarm.

The factory went crazy with bells. I rushed on to the main factory floor. 'Fire! Fire! Everybody clear the building!'

The place went wild. There's no order when there's a fire about.

I dashed downstairs, flung open the door to the boiler-room, lobbed a thirty-second grenade into the pool of oil. Then I made my way to the outer yard.

On the way I tossed the second grenade into a delivery bay, where two hundred long rolls of nylon had just been delivered. For once the muse of forlorn but plucky causes was smiling on our venture.

I dashed into the fresh air.

God, it was a stampede. People were spewing out all over the place.

But there wasn't any panic, just a sense of alarm and curiosity. They needed to be terrified.

The grenade which went off in the boiler-room saw to that. Poomph! And suddenly everyone was frozen rigid for an instant, while they took in what was happening.

Then the place took off. It was bloody chaos.

But still not enough, the warders still had it under control, herding the cons into the far end of the yard and keeping them covered. I could see Rachel in there with them, holding on to Gay's hand; as close to the gates as they could get; but a million miles from freedom.

The second grenade went off, and people were looking upward, thinking maybe we were being bombed.

I dashed into the middle of the yard. 'Clear the area!' I yelled. 'Clear the area! Bombs!' But I don't think anyone listened to me in all the pandemonium.

But I could hear someone shouting for the hoses. And then it suddenly dawned on me, I was the bloody caretaker! I was supposed to be helping fight the fire! They'd be looking for me! I couldn't just stand there. But I did. I stood there in a turmoil while people milled all around me, looking desperately across to where Gay and Rachel stared helplessly back, shepherded by half a dozen armed guards. I'd created a panic, but it wasn't enough. We were still all trapped in the factory yard.

God, I didn't know what to do. It was all going wrong. It hadn't worked at all and we were bound to be discovered.

If there were gods above and they favoured the little guys, then now was the time to help!

Suddenly there was a commotion over at the gates. It was Harry, crashing through the steel-mesh barrier like some prohibition cowboy; all guns blazing! And throwing grenades as he came.

Bang bang bang! – and all at once three ragged maws had been blasted into the perimeter fence, and twisted, skeletal metal was writhing.

Now there really was confusion. No one knew which way to run. I'm buggered if I did. I didn't remember this being in the script.

Harry roared past the guards on the gate, knocked one sideways with the wing of the van, sent the other scampering for cover with a burst from an automatic pistol. He wasn't really aiming at anybody, just firing into the air. But everybody scattered just the same, they didn't know.

He screeched around the yard in a cloud of dust and smoking rubber, tossing out grenades and gas canisters in all directions, and people whizzed about like rats in the face of the Deluge. World War III had come to Leighton Buzzard! I screamed at him, 'Get out of here you crazy bastard, they'll kill you!'

But, in truth, in the bedlam Harry had created they would have had a job even to hit him. And already people were beginning to keel over under the seduction of the gas, and a determined mob was battling towards the breached fence.

The noise was deafening, it sounded as if hell itself had opened its jaws and the damned were screaming. Like a rising tide it beat and roared about the walls, crashing and breaking and swamping us with spray.

I pulled out the last two grenades, underhanded them at an unguarded section of the fence, then ran towards Gay, clawing a way past the madding crowd, swimming through a quagmire of roiling bodies. I ripped off my shirt to clamp it over my face; wraiths of orange oblivion were writhing carelessly wherever they found a draught.

Rachel was tugging Gay towards the shattered gates, her blue cap clamped to her nose. But Gay, not understanding what the hell was going on, was pulling in the other direction, towards me. 'No!' Rachel screamed. 'Leave him! We have to go now!'

All at once the trusty blue van appeared, like a plough through the throng. It crunched to a halt in front of Rachel who squealed excitedly. She whipped Gay around and bundled her through the door, scrambled halfway in herself, clung on shrieking as the van screeched away. A couple more grenades came flying out of the window.

But I was being pressed in the opposite direction, a powerless steed ridden artlessly by the ascending terror. I struggled ferociously to break free of the torrent, but my arms were impuissant weapons, harmlessly brandished in the face of the rampant monster. In the end I had to turn and run from it, away from the gas, away from the factory which was beginning to smoke and murmur ominously.

Then the guards began to fire, as inevitably they must. Not with any care or discrimination, but everywhere, at anyone. Bullets whined in their insanity. Bloody flowers spotted the scene like poppies. And the screaming took on a new dimension, the piercing animalistic quality of voices stripped by agony. A strangely inhuman sound.

Somebody slugged me in the belly for no reason; but some people are like that. I stumbled along the factory wall for a few yards until my breath caught me up. For a ghastly second, as I listened to the crack of rifles, the wounded screams, I wondered what the fuck we had started. But this was no place to air your doubts; I had to save my skin.

I could hear Harry calling for me, somewhere. Which was a relief; in all the excitement I might have been overlooked. For such a generally quiet guy he has a hell of a voice when need demands. The only thing he forgot was to tell me where he was, it's no good just shouting Beekay! Beekay! My sense of direction falls to pieces in a panic.

When bloody holes burst amongst the bodies like raindrops in calescent ashes, the mood of the mob changed. The air of initial panic gave way to rage. All at once there was a menace which could be balanced, touched and rebated, unlike the anonymous bombs and flames of the enigmatic factory. The murderous, frightened firing of the warders was confirmation of their enmity.

All of a sudden two or three of the warders went down, ripped to the ground by the bestial claws of the canaille. Desultory terror found a surmountable focus.

And at the same time the drifting gas really began to take effect. Scores of people dropped like harvest. I started to choke, stumbled in the vague direction of the gates; though people were escaping from half a dozen holes now.

Barrels of chemicals in the factory began to explode with numbing, pounding reports, like some devilish drumbeat. A thick, rubbery smoke billowed from the first-floor windows like blood from a slashed throat. It was like bloody Ragnarok.

Could hardly see for smoke. Blundered on, straight into the little blue van which was tearing around looking for me. Harry slammed the brakes and I kind of leapt into the air, rolling across the bonnet in very undignified fashion. 'You crazy bugger!' I gasped.

I tumbled off the roof like a bundle of newspapers, flung open the rear doors as the van moved impatiently forward.

The terrified caretaker Dago ogled me wildly, trussed as neatly as a beetle in a web. Poor guy must have been bursting, it seemed an act of mercy to roll him out and crash in in his place.

I pitched on my face choking, even as the van roared away with a great lurch. We careered through a bank of tortured smoke like a chariot on a battlefield, weaving to left and right to clear the falling bodies. We bounced over the battered gates at thirty miles an hour, skittered into the road like a stone on a pond, crashed into a bevy of guards charging from the compound opposite. Some of them were still pulling their trousers up. The buggers opened fire on us.

The din in the van was unearthly, shouting and cursing came from all directions. But I was surprisingly calm. I think it was the effects of the gas. Harry threw a gun in the back, the Steyr I think, and I blasted away at the pursuit party like I was Jesse James. Whoever she is. The only problem was, my eyes were watering so much with all the gas, I couldn't see anything. But what the hell? Take that you devils!

We went tearing down the road, slewing all over the place to try to dodge the bullets. I started slinging out grenades and gas like a thing gone wild, and pretty soon the road behind was lost under vomiting pillars of fire and phantoms of swirling smoke.

From the corner of my eye I saw Rachel hanging out of the front passenger window, blazing away with a sub-machine gun. And all the time Gay kept shouting,

'Beak you're going to fall out! You're going to fall out!'
She was right too, the way Harry was driving even the
back wheels had a job holding on. I scrambled to the
front of the van and she held on to the scruff of my
neck.

But suddenly something happened. The van gave a
kick, jumped, slowed down as if an anchor had been
thrown out. We swung in a couple of wide arcs from
one side of the road to the other, waltzing about in
some crazy, lamentable performance. A lampstandard
lunged into the way and we hit it with a great crunch.
Harry twisted sideways and sprayed us all with red, and
I saw a band of blood like a sash around his neck. A
goddam bullet had ploughed through his throat.

For a moment everything was quiet as the engine
spluttered and died and water started spilling out,
hissing everywhere.

We stared at Harry with a kind of disbelief, and
Rachel burst into tears and pulled him into her lap. I
didn't know what to do. I thought we were going to
make it, and now we weren't.

I grabbed hold of Harry and pulled him off Rachel.
'Is he dead? Is he dead?' she screamed.

'Of course he's not dead you stupid bugger!'
Honestly, what sort of language is that to use? But I was
so upset. I was really stunned.

People behind us kept shooting at us. We had to get
out of here. I stuck some guns in their hands. 'Get out!
Get out! Run!'

'Don't be stupid!' one of them started to protest. But
I pushed them through the door. 'Get out, get out!
They'll bloody kill us!' They would too, they weren't
half annoyed.

The two girls stumbled out and stood there helplessly, wondering what to do. 'Beat it! Beat it!' I yelled, but they hung around waiting for me.

I tumbled into the front seat. 'For chrissake will you go! We've got to split up!'

Rachel seemed to come back to life, she started backing away in a kind of half-run, reloading as she went, pulling Gay along with her. She let them have a couple of bursts, cut across the road towards a hedge. Gay struggled with the safety on a pistol. Her hands were so cut up by the work she'd been doing she could hardly hold the damn thing. They were like an old woman's hands, and full of wounds.

I scrambled out and dragged Harry after me. God he was heavy, and he's only a little bloke. I heaved him up onto my shoulders, and he started bleeding all down my side. 'Harry! Harry! Are you awake?' He didn't answer.

I grabbed a couple of guns. Oh God he was heavy! I lumbered off, a different direction to the girls. They had to look after themselves now. Not that I'd been doing them much good anyway. I saw them disappear through the hedge and head for a housing estate.

I turned into a side road and hobbled along as fast as I could go. Harry was killing me. He was hanging down like a sack of rubber bones. There was blood all over the place. I was really desperate.

It was very quiet in this street. Everyone was peeping very discreetly from their lace curtains. I wouldn't mind living here I thought, until I trod in some dog shit. God, I'm always treading in stuff like that. Then I tripped over the pavement and nearly split my head open on someone's gate.

A young prison guard who could run faster than the rest appeared at the corner and I shot him in the belly. It was a good shot that. He doubled up and started crawling along the gutter. He must have lost something.

I struggled upward, picked Harry up again. Well, I didn't exactly pick him up. I kind of wriggled underneath him, and off we went.

We seemed to be heading for the country. The houses were getting further apart.

A dog started to chase me. I had to kick it in the face to get rid of it. I like animals, I really do. But not when they've got the leg of my goddam trousers in their mouth. I heard a lot of shouting behind me, and the sound of a motorbike, but I couldn't turn round. It was really difficult to hold on to everything, and in fact I dropped the machine gun and couldn't pick it up again. I had to leave it. I was really knackered.

Bullets started whizzing about and I had to cut down someone's garden path. Nice dahlias they had. Shame I trampled them all.

We went through a gate, across a lawn, over a fence into a field. It was sloping away below us into a stream, and there was a railway running along one side. There were sheds and a siding. I headed for them.

I was staggering about and yelling and crying. I was better than Harry though; he wasn't making any noise, but he was bleeding like hell.

We bundled over another fence and slid down a bank. A couple of hundred yards behind, ominous uniforms were spilling onto the field and fanning out.

I couldn't believe it when this train appeared round a bend – a line of empty trucks and bogeys slowly clanking along behind an ancient engine that had tried to camouflage itself with years and years of black, oily muck. It was so dirty it didn't have window wipers, just a couple of chisels. But it looked great, and I hobbled along to meet it with the speed of all my legs. Which wasn't a lot.

I wheezed past the chunking engine and set my sights on a long flat truck that was only a few feet off the rails. It came up with agonizing slowness. Actually it was quite fast, but when you can hear the shouts of the hunting party, it's pretty agonizing.

It drew level. I heaved Harry up, nearly buckled as his weight slumped back towards me, stumbled alongside desperately trying to shove him on. The stubborn bastard was determined to roll off. It's a wonder he survived his childhood, he seemed to have a bloody death wish.

At last he went. I unslung the Steyr from around my neck and tossed it on, swung myself after it.

With all the fluency of an explosion in a coathanger factory, I muffed it completely. My knee smashed against the side of the bogey and the whole leg went numb. I started to fall backwards, lost my hold, and the next second I'm being dragged along upside down with my other foot wrapped up in this stupid cable that was running down the side. All the blood rushed to my head, and started to leak out.

I managed to kick free and landed on the stones in a great heap of bruises and scraped knees. The train chugged off without me.

Hey! I picked most of me up and stumbled off in pursuit, wiping my running nose on my sleeve. It was only a little way in front, but I couldn't get there. I just couldn't go any faster. I was jiggered.

Then it stopped. The train stopped, and up ahead, the driver's head poked out to look back. He just carried on staring as I staggered alongside the train. He was just watching me. Probably impressed by my style.

I got up to the engine, wheezing and dying and dribbling, and my nose wouldn't stop running. 'What the hell's going on?' said the guy.

'Railway Inspectors,' I croaked and pulling a pistol from my belt I hauled myself up the footholds into the cab. I bet he wished he hadn't stopped now. He backed away into a corner. Except there were no corners, but he backed away anyway. God my head was pounding!

'Come on!' I commanded in a squeaky voice, and I tried to focus the pistol on him but it was difficult because I was sliding down the wall. My legs had given up. 'Move the fucking thing will you!'

White as Aunty Mel's buttocks, he pushed a few buttons and twiddled a few what's-its and the train shuddered miserably and crept forward. It was a really unhappy train. Every bone in its body creaked. I looked out, crawled to the doorway and peered back.

Way back down the track, about a quarter mile or so, a group of guards were looking after me, smoking away with their rifles. Bullets were pinging off the train all over the place.

When I turned back I was alone. That ratfink driver had jumped out the other door! And the train was slowing down.

I pulled myself up and started stabbing at buttons and fiddling all the knobs. The lights came on. The heater came on. The bloody radio came on! Finally, after about two months, we started to move again. Backwards!

'Oh God! Oh Christ!' I hopped to the doorway and squinted out. The guards were diving for cover in all directions. Ha! Boy had this confused them!

It was bloody confusing me too!

I slammed the doors shut and cowered under the

driver's seat. Pow pow pow! All the windows shot out! Holes punched themselves into the doors. The driver's packet of sandwiches blew up. I huddled on the floor screaming. Pow pow pow! Flaming bullets all over the place? It was like living in a wasp nest. I wanted Harry to come and save me. But Harry was out of it.

Son of a bitch! What else could go wrong?

It's a good job that train couldn't move very fast, otherwise, when we backed into those other trucks, there would have been a hell of a mess.

As it was, everything in sight just got smashed to bits. Two trains fighting like cat and dog. What a mess.

I think ours won. At least it ended up on top. When I looked out of the window, I was about forty feet in the air. And bits of wheel and track, wood and metal, were strewn all over the place, like a toybox had been sick.

The noise was horrendous. Like a rusty robot cleaning its teeth. I saw Harry lying at the side of the track. He'd had the sense to fall off when he saw what was coming. Not me, I was upside down with my toes in my ear. Blood was pouring out of my nose or my head or somewhere and my pants were wet. I really don't make a good accident victim.

I couldn't even find a door, everything was so mixed up. Finally I kicked off a panel in the roof and tumbled out.

The ground broke my fall.

And just about everything else by the feel of it.

For a minute I couldn't move. I just lay there, trying to breathe. There were pains everywhere. It was like being vasectomized without anaesthetic.

I started to cry, or carried on crying, I can't

remember now. I was truly in a lot of pain. My body hurt me so much, it almost made me deaf.

But I heard people running towards me. Boots crunching on the sharp grey stones. The clicks and clinks of lethal weapons. The grunting staccato of military orders.

'Get up!' someone said. 'Get up.'

Get up! I couldn't even look up. Couldn't the fool see I was in twenty pieces? Can't you see I'm fucking buggered, I said to myself. But he kicked me in the ribs.

I looked up, but I couldn't see a lot. Finally I pushed myself up on my hands, tried to blink the muck out of my eyes. The bastard slugged me in the face with the butt of his rifle. That was about the end of it.

SEVENTEEN

About half an hour later I woke up.

Nothing much had changed, except my left eye was closed and there were holes where some of my teeth used to be. Apart from that I felt great. It was just like being tortured.

I tried to move but they had me trussed up at the back. I think they'd even handcuffed my ears together. I don't know who they thought I was.

I was still lying on my face, and they were sitting round on boxes and bits of broken train. We were waiting for a van to come and collect us. That can take anything from a couple of hours to never.

Not that I was in any great hurry. I didn't suppose there'd be a surprise party for me at the other end.

It was nearly evening when it finally turned up, and I'd had to wet myself cos they wouldn't let me have a pee. They threw me in the back alongside Harry, who was almost conscious by then. But he didn't look to be in a very good way. Mind you, I don't suppose I'd make the *corps de ballet* myself. I'd frighten all the little girls to death.

Oh God I felt sick. Sick, sick, sick. What a bloody catastrophe.

Still, I suppose I did get to smash a train up. And some of it was quite exciting at the time.

It's just a pity we didn't get away with it. Shit.

So here I am, sitting in the old slammer, choking on my choky.

Harry's out of hospital now. I had a little note from his nurse. But I don't know where he is. One of the northern prisons I think.

And I'm not entirely sure what happened to the girls. I read a few newspaper reports, but they were a bit confusing. It seems Gay may have got away entirely. So did hundreds of other people. That's bloody ironic, isn't it?

Rachel created hell. She shot up dustcarts and houses, motorbike cops, cows, wood pigeons, telegraph poles, streetlights – she had a ball! They only caught her when she hijacked a rag-and-bone man and the wheel came off his cart.

She's in the nick somewhere.

Ah me. So it ends. Thing is though, if I could just get out of here, I've got this great plan worked out! I've figured out what we did wrong last time.

Only trouble is, there's this eighteen foot high wall all round me, with barbed wire and dogs and things.

But if I could just get out. See, we've still got the money! We buried it on that hilltop, under the dappling trees. We could get to America yet.

Might take me a while to figure out the details of course. And there is something else that bothers me.

See, it was my birthday the other day, and I got this card.

From Homer.

*On the following pages are details of Arrow
books that will be of interest.*

A NURSE IN TIME

Evelyn Prentis

'I've been giving it a bit of thought. I don't reckon much on your idea of being a teacher. You'd be a lot better off as a nurse . . . Besides which, nursing is more ladylike . . .'

For young Evelyn Prentis, living in 1934 on a smallholding in Lincolnshire, a new world was opened by her mother's advice – the world of nursing. Enrolling as a £25 a year trainee she started work at a busy hospital in Nottingham.

A Nurse in Time is her affectionate and funny account of the hilarity and hardship of those days, when life depended on Ovaltine, late passes and a pack of Woodbines.

'Perceptive, warm and very funny' *Sunday Telegraph*

1985

Anthony Burgess

Ingenious, chilling and darkly comic, *1985* combines a devastating critique of Orwell's *1984* with a terrifying vision of the future. As memorable as *A Clockwork Orange*, it is as powerful and unsettling as anything Burgess has written.

'Fully demonstrates Burgess's brilliance' *Francis King, Spectator*

'A book as important as it is frightening' *Daily Telegraph*

'There is too much which is truly excellent for anyone to ignore it' *Auberon Waugh, Evening Standard*

SONGS FROM THE STARS

Norman Spinrad

He was Clear Blue Lou, perfect master of the Clear Blue Way, at one with the law of muscle, sun, wind and water governing Aquaria. She was Sunshine Sue, always in a hurry in a world that was too slow, Queen of Word of Mouth. Their meeting had been arranged, their fates had been linked – but by whom? and why?

Beyond the beginning of where the world ended, beyond the highest peaks of its primeval majesty, lay a radioactive hell and the lairs of the black sorcerers, the Spacers. The black scientists had not forgotten man's old dream of touching the stars: they wanted the Age of Space reborn. But they needed a little help. . . .

'Spinrad's excitingly unique imagination at its best!'
Gene Roddenberry

'Dense and meaty, multi-levelled . . . Spinrad leads the reader gently toward wider and more awesome vistas, expanding his mind as he goes.' *Larry Niven*

BLACK EASTER
and
THE DAY AFTER JUDGEMENT

James Blish

'Each of the opposing sides in any war always predicts victory.'

Armageddon has arrived, through the offices of a megalomaniac arms dealer and an over-ambitious black magician. In one apocalyptic night, the major and minor devils are unleashed on the world. God is vanquished. And the City of Hell appears in Death Valley.

'Tremendous excitement. Black science fiction at its very best' *Time Out*

'Powerful and chilling' *Times Literary Supplement*

BAPTISM OF BLOOD

K. N. Kostov

Traitors, reactionaries, pimps, whoremasters, black marketeers, murderers and perverts – the worst the labour camp had to offer . . . they called them the gulag rats.

Punishment Battalion 333 was the roughest, wildest band of fighting men ever to draw blood. Yet they fought like the hounds of hell.

Driven by an embittered and sadistic commander against the Nazi push towards Moscow, the gulag rats face a desperate conflict of fury and brutality: their baptism of blood.

COTTON'S WAR

John Harris

If it hadn't been for the shopkeeper in Heraklion, Cotton might never have been involved . . .

In the spring of 1941 the Nazis were storming their way through Greece. The *Loukia* was crucial to the British cause and the Greek resistance – and her cargo even more so. When the *Loukia* is wrecked in enemy territory, the British gathered together a handful of 'volunteers' for a dangerous mission of retrieval: two RASC men, some sailors, one German-speaking airman and Mihale Andoni Cotonou – otherwise known as Corporal Cotton of the Marines.

A superb story of action and character, *Cotton's War* is one of John Harris's most exciting war novels.

ARMY OF SHADOWS

John Harris

France – Winter 1944. The long-awaited liberation is at hand.

The bombing mission had gone well. The crew of the Lancaster bomber began to relax. Then the Messerschmitt came out of the darkness, its guns blazing.

Of the nine-man crew only Neville and Urquhart survived, parachuting into the heart of occupied France. Now, for both of them, the testing time had begun: a time of peril as the fliers joined forces with the Army of Shadows – the men of the French Resistance – and entered a deadly game of cat and mouse with a ruthless and desperate enemy.

'John Harris writes about war as few men can. . . . With gathering speed, the story moves to a thundering climax – and a cracking good read it makes' *Daily Mail*

BESTSELLING WAR BOOKS FROM ARROW

All these books are available from your bookshop or newsagent or you can order them direct. Just tick the titles you want and complete the form below.

☐	PROUD WATERS	Ewart Brookes	£1.25
☐	A RUMOR OF WAR	Philip Caputo	£1.95
☐	ARMY OF SHADOWS	John Harris	£1.50
☐	NORTH STRIKE	John Harris	£1.50
☐	TOLL FOR THE BRAVE	Jack Higgins	£1.75
☐	THE PHOENIX ASSAULT	John Kerrigan	95p
☐	BAPTISM OF BLOOD	K. N. Kostov	£1.25
☐	THE BERLIN BUNKER	J. P. O'Donnell	£1.50
☐	STRIKE FROM THE SEA	Douglas Reeman	£1.50
☐	WITH BLOOD AND IRON	Douglas Reeman	£1.60
☐	TORPEDO RUN	Douglas Reeman	£1.50
☐	GO IN AND SINK	Douglas Reeman	£1.75
☐	DEATH OF A DIVISION	Charles Whiting	75p
☐	SS WEREWOLF	Charles Whiting	£1.50
		Postage	____
		Total	____

ARROW BOOKS, BOOKSERVICE BY POST, PO BOX 29, DOUGLAS, ISLE OF MAN, BRITISH ISLES

Please enclose a cheque or postal order made out to Arrow Books Ltd for the amount due including 15p per book for postage and packing both for orders within the UK and for overseas orders.

Please print clearly

NAME ....

ADDRESS ....

....

Whilst every effort is made to keep prices down and to keep popular books in print, Arrow Books cannot guarantee that prices will be the same as those advertised here or that the books will be available.